SMOKERS

AMIRHOSSEIN SHAHRI

DEDICATION

FIRST, I WANTED TO THANK MR. BEIGZADEH FOR TRANSLATING MY STORY AND MR. GRANT TO HELP WITH EDITING. THIS IS GOING TO BE STORY SERIES IN DIFFERENT GENRES AND FIVE CHAPTERS. SMOKERS IS CHAPTER ONE. I DEDICATE THIS BOOK TO MY MOTHER WHO IS WATCHING ME FROM HEAVEN.

AMIR

CONTENTS

Writer: Amirhossein Shahri
Translator: Majid Beigzadeh
Editor: James Grant
Cover design: Amirhossein Shahri

DAWN

"It's dawn. It's a damned dawn. The same dawn I always wished to see one day! I thought I'd begin a nice day by seeing the dawn, but this time, having seen the dawn, I finished my night all over filled with nightmare. In fact, not only my night, but my whole life! I've no idea how I got to this point, but I know I hate dawn. I hate this damned dawn till my last breath!"

In the interrogation room…

At the visiting room of the Missouri State prison, a female news correspondent with a round face, bright appearance, curly brown hair, and average build was sitting in front of Amir Shahri, a twenty-five-year-old inmate. Amir—a tall and fairly slim young man with brown, mysterious eyes—had spent the last ten years in a cell. "These are the same words you continuously repeated before you were arrested. I have heard that you carved them on the wall of your prison cell. What do you exactly mean by these words? I would like to know why you despise dawn," said the woman.

'Well, the words can assume many different meanings,' Amir exclaimed after staring at the woman. 'It matters which ones you are referring to, Miss...?' His pause was understood, as the correspondent interjected with 'Jill Fain.'

'Oh, yes, Jill! I've never been good at keeping names in mind, but that does not matter much. What is of importance here is the fact that what you can, as I said, perceive those words in numerous ways,' said Amir.

'How did you feel when you were frantically repeating those words? After all, they were excessively dark and weird to hear from a young man,' Jill stated. Amir interrupted her at once and said, 'I prefer the word "weird." After all these years, I am a devilish guy to many people, but the truth is I just want to be different! I look weird to them, and this is what I wished to be!'

'So, everything that happened was a consequence of your longing to appear weird?' Jill asked.

'Weird, different, peculiar! All of them may suggest a similar meaning. You know, Jill, language is very complicated. You can displace a few words and their meanings and displace the whole world as a result. This is certainly something evident for a reporter like you, correct?'

'Maybe the words can substitute each other, but human deeds have no substitution. One's actions oftentimes cannot be understood in multiple ways," Jill said.

'Don't misunderstand! I'm not here because others couldn't bond with me. Instead, I'm here simply because no one could appreciate my uniqueness—but that matters no more. In response to your question about my current feelings, let me ask if you were ever fond of a childhood toy or doll that lost its appeal because you grew up and achieved your dreams' Amir said with a smile.

'Yes! That has happened to me several times,' Jill promptly

2

replied.

'Did you ever ask yourself why?' Amir asked.

'Maybe some things look beautiful through different lenses but aren't what they appear to be when scrutinized from different perspectives,' said Jill.

'Interesting comment!' Amir replied. 'But I think it's mostly because at that moment—at that single point in time—you long for that item, but when you get it after a long period of waiting, it doesn't look as attractive as when you first saw it. This is why I think it's better to forget things you are not able to quickly attain! When I was younger, I wished to see the dawn, but I no longer do because it has lost its appeal to me!' Amir revealed.

'Perhaps the moment when you had reached the deadline, you weren't happy even though you achieved your greatest wish! Did you achieve your greatest wish?' asked Jill. Amir frowned a little and said indifferently, 'I don't think so! You may not be able to control your inner feelings. Suppose you are being tortured, having your limbs dragged to every side. Even in that situation, your favorite song being played would give you a nice feeling, though very slight and transient. Your body wouldn't say, 'now that you're dying under torture, I won't secrete any hormones because hearing a song can't help!' The body performs its duty. At least, for a moment, I should have gained a positive feeling by seeing the dawn. However, I felt so indifferent; it was as if the national anthem of China was being played for me!'

Jill smiled a little, making Amir change his dull mood. A shaky smile on Amir's face lessened the dreary atmosphere in the room.

'Of course, you are still admired as a hero by a group of people.' Jill said.

3

'Well, this is the nature of the world: any incident—wrong or unfavorable—may have positive outcomes,' Amir explained.

'For example, what?' Jill asked.

Amir, pointing to himself, said 'Smokers!'

Jill smiled a little, nodded and said: 'Other than smokers.' Amir stared at the corner of the room and answered after a while by saying, 'Consider Adam and Eve eating the apple. Had they not made their mistake, we wouldn't have found the chance to sit in front of each other!'

'Are you a believer?' Jill asked.

'Not such an unbeliever!' Amir asserted.

'How come a believer reaches to smokers at the end of his way?' Jill asked.

'The human being is a flexible creature! The fate of man can be changed at any moment. Would you have predicted being here ten years ago?" Amir asked. Jill nodded her head in agreeance and said, 'Yes! Since then, however, many things have changed. Please explain the very moment that caused you to be here.' Amir took a brief look at the ceiling, bit his lip, and thoughtfully said, 'I don't exactly remember which one caused the biggest change. The story of smokers had its ups and downs, and no moment was powerful enough to change everything by itself; there were many significant events happenings. Which one do you intend to choose for your journal?'

'What if you start from the beginning, where all your fateful moments are?' Jill asked. Amir shrugged and said, 'Throughout the day, I review my whole story in such a way that I can make a precise movie. Today's review, I will share with you!

'Why do you think so much about it? Is it the stab of guilt?' Jill

4

asked.

'That is the point! I review it to decide if I deserve the stab; I don't know if I was the protagonist or the antagonist. I simply know that I was different!' Amir replied.

Jill reached into her purse and took out the cassette tape and asked for permission to record by saying, 'No problem if I record our talk, correct?' Amir allusively looked at her and said, 'Ten years have passed since my trial. I don't think I can make things worse for me, and nothing left to be used against me is hidden!' Jill turned on the recorder while Amir shuffled around on the chair a little, paused, and sternly said, 'I'm Amir Shahri, the founder of smokers!'

NOT A TYPICAL BOY

I n the story…

A revolution occurred in my country early in 1979, so I
went to Missouri with my family. I was four at that
time; thus, I have no special memory of the times
before. I was the only child of the family. My father
began his job at the post office shortly after we arrived—we
did not have a good economic situation when we moved to
Rolla.

Though we found ourselves initially struggling in Rolla, the
town attracted us for two reasons: First, it was a small city that
would make it easy for us to get used to a new culture; second,
living expenses were far lower in comparison with larger cities.
While I enjoyed my time there, something incessantly bothered
me: The population of about 20,000 people made it difficult
for strangers to become known and popular because anything
out of the ordinary was deemed as "different."

For example, two guys and I were the only ones with a
different religion than the majority of people living in the city.
For me, it was somehow more difficult to communicate with

others. There were neither countrymen nor persons speaking our language. Of course, because I had arrived in the US at a young age, it was easy for me to learn English; because of this, I did not have much trouble speaking it.

My family, however, didn't share my story. My father began learning English just before immigrating to the US and had considerable progress but still had communication issues; my mother had much trouble learning English, which caused her to lose self-confidence. On one hand, she couldn't find a proper job in the city, as she was not, as mentioned, a fluent English speaker. On the other hand, she did not have enough energy or expertise for jobs that didn't require adequate English skills. She gradually lost more confidence and consequently became depressed. The least I can say is that my parents didn't feel comfortable in our new town.

All of our relatives remained in our homeland, which made us feel further isolated here; this should not be mentioned without also noting that we were unsure of our future. We had entered a new stage in our life where we had no experience or anyone who could help us progress as new citizens of both the country and state. We felt alone, and this loneliness always made me ask myself, "what at last?"

Perhaps this is a question that anyone would ask themselves at any time or any place, but it was different to me. I had not lived enough in my homeland to consider returning it. I felt as if I belonged nowhere, a feeling similar to losing something and having absolutely no idea where it is despite feverish searching! Still, I had not found my question or what its answer should be! That's why I say it was different to me.

Perhaps if I was born here, or if I had spent my whole life in my homeland, and if here, and with the existing situation, I just found a few guys speaking my language, so that I could communicate without any worry or anxiety, the question would never get bold, and the word 'smokers' would never form in my mind. Please, do not think that people treated me indecently—they were courteous. It was not their behavior that created that question; instead, it was the life and happenings inside them.

Well, of course, it's natural for kids—young children and teenagers—to get in touch with their peers. They usually don't think about the consequences, but they quickly believe that they will be happy if they connect with others. Perhaps if I were in my own country, I would hardly be able to communicate with a man of a different culture or from another country. This is the nature of man, particularly in his youth or teenage years.

Like others, I had my own friends with whom I spent most of the time, but there was something within me, I didn't know what, that unsettled my tranquility. Days passed, and—like people of the city—I was busy with my routine life. Since I didn't associate myself with any social group, country, or religion, no special occasion, celebration, or date made me ecstatic.

This matter itself supported my questions, 'What's the aim of life? Why am I here now? Is it the same process of life that I had to do? Did I take the right path, or according to some, I'm doing the right thing? What at last? What is really last?'

Though I was acclimating on a daily basis, the question about the nature of my existence became increasingly ambiguous and irrational! One day when I was going from my room to the refrigerator, I was attracted by a televised interview in which a psychologist was talking about the exact issue I had always been waiting for.

The psychologist didn't answer my questions, but he showed me how to begin solving my issues during one part of the discussion! That part of the interview was about mental disorders: 'Most of the time, our spirit is suffering, and we are looking for an external or foreign cure for it; if we refer to our own conscience, we find that neither medicine nor humans can cure it. We can help treat our soul. Always remember that to have a happy life, we must start with ourselves. A heart that is dark inside will never emit external light.'

I didn't get an exact response to my question, but I found out where to find it. At the time, I was about fourteen and just started to mature; I had no idea if the things that entangled my mind were because of puberty or emotional factors that resulted from our move. For this reason, I tried to confide some of my obsessions with my friends who were about my age to find out if they had the same problems. My friends' reactions were far from what I expected.

We were all freshmen, and most of us felt somewhat like grown-ups. We liked to imitate grown-ups by putting on clothes akin to theirs, speaking as they did, and even enjoying the same activities. Well, my friends had found their behavioral patterns in advance. They knew the people to follow and what obsessions to have even if they didn't deeply believe in what they did.

Thus, no place was left for challenging their life goals or changing theirs habits. For this reason, my friends' reactions made it seem as if I had spoken to them in a foreign language. I understood I was alone in this path, and no one understood what I tried to say or what I wanted. So, I decided not to continue and avoid speaking. It's very distressing when you have such a great and important question but find no one to answer!

I never found myself so close to my parents to raise my questions. Our only talks were concerned with high-school activities and my grades. As time passed, our relationship was weakening, and the strange thing was that we only felt to belong to each other. Outside home, we didn't have an intimate friend that could replace a family member. Because I didn't belong to any group or philosophy, I inadvertently felt indifferent to my cold relationship with my family and did nothing to mend it.

The remarks of that psychologist helped me much in pursuing the answer to my questions. According to him, I did not need a psychoanalyst or a medicine. Instead, I needed to find my inner self and get a better knowledge about it. Gradually, it was getting to be a habit with me to make use of any time, even a small bit of it, to know myself better; the more I did, the more I got addicted to it! I attended gatherings only if was necessary, and if anyone didn't invite me or call my name, I wouldn't attend.

The more I thought to find about the philosophy of my existence, the more questions formed in my mind. To increase my mind efficiency, I looked everywhere to see which atmosphere helped me more with communicating with my surroundings, just like those students who change their place of study, with the hope to learn more.

Now that I think about it, I see that all that advice is ineffective! In the worst possible situation, you may have a better understanding. Well, I was fourteen at that time, and like all other human beings, I was looking for an external savior. Sometimes, I went to the library; other times, I would hide under stairs of our house. Finally, sometimes, I would hide even in nature; however, most of the time, I was busy thinking in my own room at home.

My room was a better place, because I could close the door and pull my room's curtains to ensure no one could see me. When I went out, I used to take a few books with me and pretended to read so that no one would think I had gone insane.

I had a small notebook, where I quickly jotted down every point I found out about my personality traits. I usually put the

10

notebook inside the drawer of my reading desk so when my mother went to my room for cleaning, she wouldn't throw them away as trash by mistake.

Nevertheless, since these notes were the exact hidden points of my personality, I would feel naked if someone read them, and I always felt like someone was watching me! The notes were the most personal things I had in my whole life.

The first days, I reached no peculiar points. As I had become more sensitive to who I really was, however, I began quickly memorizing what happened daily and wrote it down somewhere. Then I would think about my behavior indifferently to find out why I had done so.

When I was certain about the reason or confident that I knew what was happening, I wrote it down on the notepaper, or when I settled in similar situations several times, I could find out the main reason for my behavior by comparing my reactions. Well, some of them were like those of others, which seemed natural.

For example, when I saw my female classmates looking at me, my energy and concentration increased at that moment. I don't know how or why, but I later realized that the rest of the guys had similar behaviors. I avoided writing down the similarities between my friends and I because these points doing same thing so would have been of no benefit. If my behavior could have such an effect, then the others who shared that behavior should have my obsessions.

They were so indifferent to the question 'what at last?' Therefore, I had to pursue those points in my personality that no one had so I could find the very answer to the question that no one had! In the beginning—as the question was very philosophical, important, and fundamental—I decided to find viewpoints of great psychologists, philosophers, and mystics in this regard to help me start looking for my inner self, but I encountered two problems.

First, I didn't have enough capacity to perceive those sophisticated articles and books—they were somehow beyond my understanding. Second, after a while, I felt that it was not Amir who was looking at those challenges and problems in a broader sense but philosophers who directed vision and thought.

I decided to stop reading the books written in relation with my question and not speak even a word with anybody in this regard because in the first years of adolescence, human being possesses a flexible personality and weak conception. I was looking for my original self, so I had to use an indifferent and neutral perspective so that I could release myself from the complexities of my mind. I shouldn't view the world through the eyes of others or align my life according to their mentality to find answers to my questions.

I had become totally isolated, but I had neither a warm relationship with my family nor a noteworthy personality at school. My mother had made friends with a few of neighbors. They had started to invite each other over for coffee. Not to feel ashamed before other Mesdames, my mother exercised English more than before and was careful about the customs and etiquette of others so she could be like them.

My father, too, had become more acquainted with a few of his colleagues and invited them over for dinner or was invited by them. My friends were just living to experience the same things they couldn't experience when they were younger and had to wait till they grew up more. In the middle of this, I was the only one whose presence was not felt. I had no complaint either, as I was busy exploring myself.

Well, there was some breakthrough. For example, I often could conceive my feeling, when I did not have a good sense, and at the same moment, I could understand the reason behind my mental distress.

After a long time of exercising this approach, my unconscious mind was vigilantly ready to record the moments and explore the reasons behind my feelings. One day when I was returning home from school, I got a bad feeling for no reason. This time, I didn't let that feeling go; I stood abruptly and started to think about the last moment I remembered, just like a filmstrip we rewind to watch any scene from a movie.

I carried on and reached the few minutes ahead when I passed by a bar and saw a schoolmate girl who seemed so cute, at least to me, and always drew my attention. She was likely the girl in my dreams I wanted to be with. Her name was Susan and she was sitting in a corner, drinking beer with a guy from school three years older than us.

It's true that neither of them had reached the legal age to drink beer, but Rolla was a small city, and one of the local bars unofficially sold beer to people under legal age. I had heard this before, but I was not bothered by it. What made me upset was that I didn't understand why that girl was always uninterested in me even though I had tried several times to draw her attention in class.

I had a feeling that the only reason the girl drew closer to the boy was because of the beer. I couldn't drink beer because my religious beliefs did not allow me to and because I was not prone to breaking the law—I had a sense of discipline. I was always afraid of breaking norms, but my favorite part of the newspaper was the incident pages.

Wow! Right now, I have reached another contradiction! I was busy trying to find out where my bad feelings had originated from but realized a deeper challenge! It was like having one dream, waking up, and having another!

One would say that I was detached from my matrix and didn't

understand that for ten minutes, I had stood on the street, staring at a corner as if I was spell-bound. I came to myself. My first challenge was obvious: I was upset because I had seen my favorite girl with a guy. Poor Amir! My second and more important challenge came from the fact that a part of my existence always refuses something, while the other part is continuously absorbing it.

How come a person who hates so much breaking law may be interested in reading news bits that are nothing but the breaking of norms? I quickly returned home, took a piece of my notepaper, and added this point. I closed my bedroom door. My mother asked if I was ready for lunch, and I said that I didn't have an appetite. I sat on the chair and concentrated to remember if it ever happened to me to do the same thing before other than this example. A little bit of thinking. A little more. A little bit deeper. A little bit darker!

Oh, yes! It's right that I had no sense of dependence to any source of power or thought, but anyway I had so far kept my beliefs and faith. Perhaps I didn't do many things because of those beliefs, but I would always prefer to spend my time around people who either did or at least talked about it.

One of those things was drinking beer. Most of my friends either used to drink beer furtively or were eager for it, but I did know men who were not interested by it. Why didn't I spend my time with them? Really, why? Why, for instance, did I— someone who always feared heights—take the way home where there was a cliff of high altitude?

With no exception, I always took the same way and tried to leap down from the height. Sometimes, I made it; sometimes, I did not. Now that I think of it, I see that I took the same way home today; however, because my mind was engaged, I didn't think about it. It's odd that I'm always looking for the things I usually avoid. One would say they're two separate souls within one body. The question lies within which one of the two is my

14

conscious self.

I thought more, tried to edit my note a little, and sorted out my unique characters and the reasons behind appearing of those characters in order to explore the relationship among them. Perhaps that relationship was the key to all my mental unrest. Afterwards, I became horribly deeper and tried to examine myself minutely.

For about a month or two, beside doing my homework and studying for exams, I delved deeper into myself. At last, after all this quarantined life, I could find out the answer. In simple words, I could know myself and explore the darkest, deepest and the most hidden dimension of my personality. Supervising my life, I could divide my source personality into three pieces.

Most of my deeds and characters derived from these three parts. First, my religious beliefs, by which all my judgements on good and evil were done, and as there lived a considerable number of religious people in Rolla, I couldn't understand if it was my own way of thinking or a way that was imposed on me by the society I was living in. Second, my interest to encounter the 'must-nots.' The must-nots were created in my mind, but a part of my personality was constantly searching for them!

The third: my extreme interest to disclose the mysteries and the unknown. This character developed in me while surveying my favorite books and movies. I just loved movies, stories, and articles containing the unknown.

These three characteristics formed my triangular personality. Through this triangle, one could unveil my true nature. Now, after all the time I spent looking for these three elements, I had the key and only had to discover how to use it.

At that time, I had a feeling that a part of me was standing behind the door—a part of me that would exclaim, "How come I didn't guess it was you sooner? So, you were behind

15

this riddle!"

I just had one more step to find the relationship between the three elements. Whatever I would reach for would be my true self, which couldn't be denied or hidden! I thought about it until an idea popped into my mind. It was as if that part of me behind the door tried to help me find him as soon as possible.

I felt its existence, but I couldn't get in touch with him. The idea was trying to let my hidden emotions take control of my actions without me being capable of controlling myself, but how? It's so simple! You must set yourself on automatic mode and let the part of yourself that's always hidden take control of your body!

AQUAINTANCE WITH INNER DARKSIDE

Fearing being called foolish by others is the reason why that part of your soul is always terrified and hiding. If we don't give him an excuse to fear, he won't feel as a stranger. The less he feels danger and fear, the easier he can control the body!

I don't know how I got this idea, but it was a hard and difficult job! I had to work on my mind for hours to be able to rid myself of my feelings and thoughts. When my soul container got empty, it worked as a trap! It tempted my hidden part to steal the control room of my mind! He ran away as soon as I lost control or got excited and emotional; at that point, I had to start concentrating again!

I tried to be in solitude so that no one could disrupt my concentration. After a few weeks of struggle, I got a feeling that my mind was in standby mode, and, in a real sense, I could lose my control.

A few minutes passed, and he showed up! Well, it wasn't as if my arms started moving by themselves. The truth is that, as I didn't intend to judge, the hidden part let itself introduce its ideas to my mind. This way, I understood it was not my own idea but something outside myself, just like the very idea that showed me how to pave the way for it to introduce himself!

As I said, my aim was to find the relationship between the three personality traits, but I had to establish a strong connection with him before I could start a question and answer session. His first command was to reach and eat the whole cake inside the refrigerator! I let myself free to do whatever *he* wanted to do!

It's an odd feeling that you share your body and another soul! I didn't like to have a roommate at all. I had a bad feeling about this one. It was different than before. He ate all the cake. Oh, no! *I* ate the whole cake! It was me who ate the cake. I had control of all my body parts, but he was the one who issued commands!

My room was on the second floor. I thought *he* would tell me to turn on the TV and watch such and such, but it seemed *he* was not so shy! *He* ordered me to open the window, so I did. *He* said, "Jump!" I looked down. I wouldn't die if I jumped down, but it was high enough for me to fear the fall. It was as if *he* whispered directly into my ears when he ordered me to jump.

I had to obey him so I could catch him! I jumped down, something I would never do on my own. I stood up and wiped the dust off my clothes. Trying to keep calm and not to be excited was more difficult than jumping off the window. For a few weeks, I was trying to keep a neutral position, but after all it was still difficult.

I had no more time to be surprised; I shouldn't think anymore. I shouldn't make an extra move. I should empty myself of all my emotion so that *he* would have a place to boast.

A little later, *he* whispered, "School!" I really didn't want to go.

Anything could happen there, but because I would not let him judge me for my fear, I carried on with a mind void of hesitation. On my way to school, I saw a few of my classmates who said, "Hey, Amir! The guys have got some beer. We're going to a friend's backyard to have a little fun. Susan is with us!"

I was about to accept the invite, but I shouldn't have any presupposition to know what the other side of me desired. *He* surprised me, as a firm 'No' came from his mouth. They thought I would go to hell for the sake of Susan, but I just passed by in a cold, serious mood. When I arrived at school, I saw a few of the guys playing football. Indeed, most of them played much better than me.

He said, "Play!" Perhaps I would never have wanted to play with them, but I expected worse than that. It was just a game. It couldn't be so bad. I didn't want to think what *he* meant by that, otherwise *he* would probably sense danger and stop controlling me. I started to play. After a few minutes, it wasn't me who played but *him*!

I was playing so smoothly. I started to perform a few technical moves that I used to do in my own exercises, but as I was not so skilled, I didn't dare perform them much in front of others. Nevertheless, things were progressing well, and the guys were surprised. My play was not bad overall, which made me happy.

A few dreamlike minutes passed and I was playing phenomenal. I even thought that perhaps, a superman existed within me and that I can easily allow him to bring me success while I look and enjoy life. Soon, I understood that I was making a mistake. The ball stumbled under my foot, and I fell. I told myself it was an accident. A few moments later, when I was performing a skilled move, an opposing player captured the ball. I was not quick enough, my body couldn't resist, and I, as said, fell.

Very soon, I returned to reality. My bad play continued until my teammates yelled at me for frequently coughing up the ball. I decided to perform simpler moves, but *he* didn't allow! Every time I received the ball, I did the same things that I didn't dare do during real play. Now I was coughing up the ball so often that I decided to leave the game.

He told me, "Don't leave the game!" I paid no attention and went back home. The next day, I didn't have any plan to let him control my mind, but *he* showed up again in the classroom. I became alert and found myself surrounded by my classmates. I was afraid, but I remembered that I couldn't be afraid! I thought to myself that it was a long time I had been waiting for a chance like this, and I shouldn't let the golden opportunity be wasted.

In the classroom, I was entirely quiet and wouldn't talk to the teacher unless she asked me a question. I was waiting for him to surprise me, as *he* did the day before in the football game, by whispering the answer in my ears! This time, it wasn't the same. *He* just hinted at the part of my memory related to the teacher's question. If I was on my own, I could reach the part of my mind *he* hinted at but probably it would take longer! In other words, *he* had increased the speed of my mind processing time, but *he* would never let me know the answer!

Again, it jumped to my mind that this way: I didn't need to study my lessons so much because *he* would help me in my exams! In simpler words, I would help myself cheat my exams in a way no one would observe! Nevertheless, my dreams faded when I gave the wrong answer to the teacher.

Truly, when I raised my hand to answer the first two questions, I gave very good answers. My answers to the next two questions were wrong. After being quiet in the class for a few months, I had suddenly started to speak and gave answers to all the questions asked!

It seemed a little silly, and others didn't have such a positive view of me because of that. It made me feel so bad. I wished the class would finish soon. Until the end of the class, *he* repeatedly asked me to be active, but I didn't let him tempt me. Almost half the answers *he* suggested were wrong.

He felt no more a stranger to me, and as soon as *he* found me void of any thought or feeling, he showed up. Occasionally, when I was not thinking about him, he reminded me his existence! I was getting used to his presence.

A few days later, in Lab class—my least favorite class—*he*, as usual, suggested a few of his ideas. I didn't know how those ideas, some good and some bad, developed in him, but they surprised my classmates.

We were busy making a simple foam during the lab. Necessary materials to make the foam were a plastic bottle, an aluminum container for holding the bottle, a conic cap, a few drops of food coloring to be mixed with peroxide, a teaspoonful of dishwashing liquid, and a little yeast.

I had seen the way foam was made on TV before, so immediately after the teacher handed me the materials, I began making it. *He* reminded me that I had seen the same thing before, but because the memory was made a long time ago, I couldn't remember the exact amount of materials to be mixed.

The others in my group told me not to rush, but *he* insisted that I finish the job alone. I mixed the food coloring with peroxide and poured the mixture into the bottle. I then added the dishwashing liquid and the yeast to the bottle, but as I over calculated the amount of the yeast and the dishwashing liquid, the produced foam spilled onto the table.

The teacher got upset and, after browbeating our group, gave us no grades. It was all my fault. My group lost their temper and told me what they wished. One of them said, "What's your problem? You're doing silly things. Oh, I forgot that you are a chump!" I had nothing to say and was sweating and embarrassed.

I was gradually becoming disappointed with *him*. I feared being judged by others, and it caused him not to show up anymore. For the next few days *he* didn't appear, because I had become cautious and didn't let him feel free to enter my mind. I wonder if it got better or worse. In my daily life, I mostly felt his absence from within me than from outside. It was the virtue of his presence that increased my risk-taking.

I was the accused one, not him, because he didn't have an independent physical existence. All people identified me as the cause of the mistake. For a while, I canceled my program on self-analysis because it bore no fruit. Everything had gotten back to routine until he showed up a few days later, when I was having dinner with my family.

I rarely talked to my parents, especially at the dinner table. Occasionally, my father asked me about school and my grades, and I usually gave some routine answers that I really got bored of. "Well, my son, how are your grades? Is everything okay at school?" My father asked as usual.

I was about to give a routine answer when *he* showed up again and whispered an unexpected answer in my ear. As his presence had not such an impact on my life's quality, I didn't show a reaction.

However, I decided to give him another chance so that he might brag and give me a clue to a proper answer. *He* began to whisper sarcastically, "This is not the life that your father promised you five years ago!"

His whisper triggered me to answer to my father, "You can play the role of worried fathers much better than this!"

My mother tried to stop me from talking. My father, who

didn't expect such an answer, said, "Are you upset with something now?"

Thereafter, *he* issued the words, and I spoke them! Those words were not what I really meant. Although I was not opposed to such words, I didn't think on saying them. The decision was made by *him*. I felt like I was possessed by a demon, but I was too anxious to know the ending words of my father.

"Does it make any difference?" I answered to my father.

"If you have any words, be brave; say what you want to say!" My father said.

"Look who is talking of bravery," I answered.

My mother asked me to stop it, but my father interrupted her and said, "What next? I want to know how my son is raised when I'm not home." He turned to me and said, "Feel free to go on!"

I paid the least attention to him. I wonder if my indifference was because of my recent exercises to become unsympathetic or if I was indifferent to emotional issues. Anyway, in both cases, it didn't make any difference because I was satisfied with what he said.

I cleaned my mouth with a piece of tissue, took a glass of water, stared at my father, and said sarcastically, "You better talk about bravery when you don't run away to spend time with your buddies so that when you return home you will see that your son is much different with what you promised him to be!"

Frankly, it was a question for me to know what my father promised.

That was what my father asked exactly, "What promise did I make five years ago that I have now broken?"

That moment, I got a little stressed because I thought they would expect Amir, not *him,* to answer.

Before I got wet with sweat, *he* told me about a memory, when my father decided to stay in Rolla five years ago despite finding a better job somewhere else. Considering the lower expenses of life in Rolla, my father could save some money even with his low salary. My father believed that we could save enough money in one year, then leave Rolla. We couldn't, and we had to extend our stay for the next five years.

I had not thought about it even once. I've got no idea how *he* pulled it out my memory. After hearing me out, my father lost control and pounded his fist on the table. He started to mention his endeavors and devotions for the family and concluded how ungrateful I was to have only made that single statement. His face was red with anger; he cried out so loudly that it made my mother and I afraid. It seldom happens that I see my father act in such a way.

"Leave the dinner table," *he* said. I was in a bad situation: I had to see the quarrel between my father and the dark side of myself. As I was not the cause of the tangle, I let him set himself free from the trouble. I slammed the glass of water on the table and went to my room.

"I didn't let you go," my father shouted.

I stopped and as *he* whispered to my ear and said, "I don't need your permission." I said that and continued walking to my room.

My father wanted to go to my room, but my mother stopped him. She didn't like quarrels at all. It was among the reasons why we migrated from our homeland.

I closed my room's door. I was so angry. I wanted to be certain if it were me who was teasing myself or a part of me from the depth of my inner self.

In fact, it's too difficult to understand that matter for the people who are alone and think a lot. The mind becomes more creative in loneliness. That's not always fruitful because it sometimes produces bad things and makes you believe them in an odd manner. I needed to know if the hidden character within me was a product of my mind. If so, I had to find another solution to reach an answer to my question.

I stood against the wall mirror and stared into my eyes. Like the movies, I was waiting to see a different character appear. 'Alas! It happens in movies,' I said. I was so upset that all my struggle was in vain.

I reached for my note pad and stared at it once again. I lied down on my bed, took the note pad in my hand, and looked at those three main traits.

I repeated myself, "Prove yourself! Prove yourself!" After repeating for a while, I stared at my note slip and saw all pieces of the jigsaw puzzle fell into place. Again, everything faded.

I sprang up, stood in front of the mirror, and angrily said, "If you want to prove yourself, now is the time. You were waiting for a chance all this time. I let you do as you wished. Look! You have ruined my life. You damned! What do you want from me? Who are you?"

He showed up again and said, "All this time, you were looking for the answer that you knew already!"

I continued in doubt, "What answer? I wouldn't talk to you like a Schizophrenic if I knew the answer!"

Just after saying that, I became astounded and said to myself, "Maybe all these are really the result of my imagination, and I am really ill!" I remembered reading an article that claimed that about forty percent of Schizophrenia patients are left-handed! Oh, my Gosh! I'm left-handed, too!

I, scared more than before, really lost my nerve. I sat on a chair and stared at a corner. *He* began to whisper in my ear again. I sprang from the chair, put my fingers in my ears, and began cursing. I was swirling around to distract myself so *he* couldn't control my mind again.

I kept on swirling until I got tired. While gasping for breath, I sat on the floor. After a few seconds, when my heartbeat returned to normal, he said, "Note slip!" I wanted to talk again and put my fingers in my ears.

I rushed to the note slip at the corner of the room and wanted to tear it, but I happened to see the words on it. Again, a vague scene appeared to me as if all the pieces of a jigsaw puzzle fell into place and disappeared! It looked so weird; as soon as I stared at the paper, I could see that image.

I decided to look more so that I could see that image once more. For that moment, I changed my mind to tear it. I kept on looking. My memories of the few past weeks unconsciously appeared to me. Yeah! The note slip was not the clue to my questions; it was the answer itself! It introduced my hidden personality trait in the deepest part of my inner self!

I didn't need to get myself into trouble that much. I just had to look more carefully at that note slip. All things he wanted me to do were in conformity with the three personality traits that I had noted.

The first of them were my religious beliefs. I remembered that when my friends asked me to join them to drink beer, *he* didn't let me attend even though my favorite girl was there, and I didn't drink alcohol.

The second trait didn't elate me so much because *he* showed interest in the things I feared but not all of them. That's why I couldn't attribute every fear in me to *his* interest. For instance, I feared driving, so I didn't stealthily take the keys of my father's car to drive around in it. *He* never insisted to. So, *he* might have another goal that he wanted to show me by making me do a series of tasks.

The third was my interest in mysteries and exploring the hiddens. That trait was in full conformity with my favorite articles, ones oftentimes concerned with UFOs, the structure of Egyptian pyramids, the secrets of past civilizations, the mysteries of sorcery, etc. I had numerous fears in life to face, and it tempted *him* to make me challenge whatever I feared but why?

I thought some more about it. What were his goals when he made me perform technical soccer moves, do lab tests individually at school, answer the questions by the teacher, … etc.? The answer was terribly clear! No need to think about it. *He* just had desire to be seen!

My tense and frowned face turned happy and smiling. I started to laugh unwantedly—I couldn't stop laughing. Perhaps it was the happiest moment I ever had in my life. Finally, I had made it after almost a long time of struggling to trap the hidden and darkest part of my inner self.

Yeah! It's so simple. Within me, I always loved to be famous, but I used to deny it maybe because of my fear to be defeated. Surely, I couldn't get the answer automatically if I was truthful with myself if I looked at the mirror and thought about myself!

This was the hidden part of my personality that never showed up so that I could reach him even if I wanted to sincerely judge myself. I was so happy that I totally forgot my arguing with my father a few minutes earlier. Nothing could ruin my good feeling at that moment. Ultimately, I had a friend who was the closest to me, and more importantly, *he* was always beside me!

NEW ME

In that internal adventurism, the only remaining thing was to make that friend satisfied. The next day, I kept my ordinary life but without any feeling of loss. No more I looked for anything, as I had found everything I was searching for. I was in no hurry because I had heard somewhere that "understanding a question is half an answer."

Thus, I had covered half the way. I hadn't paid dearly for it, but I spent my time on it and was troubled a little. Nothing mattered anymore. I continued my life with self-confidence because I never thought about failure in reaching my goal.

Another reason why I didn't follow my goals in haste was because of the newly found part of my self always accompanied me. It couldn't get lost or be destroyed. By the way, I didn't need to repeat it to my conscious self! What I expected from *him* was already there! *He* could visit the dark depth of my soul and feed alone on what I prepared for him.

I didn't feel as if I am at his service or that he is someone other than me! We were two sides of the same coin. A one-sided coin is good for nothing! Our relationship was not that of a lord and a vassal!

The triggering question "What at last?" drove me here, and I had an answer for it! Logically, your goal to accomplish in life should be feeling satisfied but not the kind of silly satisfaction like tracking a soap opera or getting good grades at final exams! What I mean here in my winding story is a kind of deep and inner satisfaction like *his*.

To me, this inner satisfaction is something different in every person. To obtain a real peace, people should search and find the hidden part of their inner self. An important point lies here: once this conscience is awakened and active, you cannot make it inactive, and it will accompany you until your last breath! Now I understand why in some philosophical articles they say, "ignorance is sometimes better than knowledge." Sometimes, knowledge causes pain, and because awareness and consciousness never reduce to ignorance, so pain will accompany man forever!

I never ever wanted to lose that newly activated conscience. I couldn't even forget it if I wanted to. Well, having this in mind, the risk of that procedure would increase! Perhaps a person owns an anti-social and self-wanted inner self, by which they can obtain a real satisfaction. Fortunately, it was not too risky for me, but as it could be risky for others, I don't remember if I have ever raised it.

The point that the inner and hidden enthusiasm of man to something cannot be the answer to that question leaped in my mind several times. For example, in me—who is innately looking for superiority and being known—these two traits are not exact answers to the question "What at last?" Still, another question is left: say you obtained a spiritual tranquility at last, and your soul is convinced—what then?

I always looked for the last step even when the answer to my question was not the last step! That fundamental question was always there even if I obtained whatever I wished for. Well, it was the very point where my way in life separated from others. I didn't believe that money is worthless and conclude that struggling to become wealthy is pointless. To me, a wealthy person can talk about money value. Someone who has never experienced something, has no right to comment on it. So, firstly, I had to get my wish fulfilled so I could comment on whether it was the same thing I was looking for! In other words, I had to get to the last point so that I might have the permission to ask myself, "What at last?"

The same mentality changed my route in life and caused me to follow my goals and not surrender. In the meantime, I didn't want to feel that I am doing it for someone other than me. I had to get rid of the pronoun *he*! There had to be no more *he*, but *I*.

Still, there was a problem: there were some contradictions between me, who already existed, and the other person who was newly discovered in the depth of my soul! Those two selves - that I and this I- did not move on the same route! When I wanted to make any decision, I had to prefer one over the other. By the way, I had to choose a separate name for each so I could recognize them individually.

A foreign name gave me a weird feeling. Perhaps I was too sensitive, but I wanted to proceed in a way I thought it was right. I remembered to have heard my mother several times that after birth: I was to be called Hossein, and in my childhood, they used to call me Hossein but chose Amir for my id card.

I chose Hossein for *him,* though I was Amir. When I had to deal with him, I was Hossein. However, I had to carry on this acting to the point where these two characters were merged, and there was only one identity: Amirhossein! It was my little secret.

30

Now, let me tell a little about the only Amir. He was a talented and enthusiastic boy who always stared at the biggest stars. He always used to follow the best and highest values. He didn't grieve over things he didn't have, but he always moved across his great expectations, those that others perhaps considered them as their dreams. However, as I said earlier, his fear of failure possibly caused him not to pay serious attention to them.

That was the reason of my bewilderment in life. From within me, I was looking for something that Amir's cautious character didn't let it emerge. I felt lost and empty inside to the extent that the question "What at last?" was carved on my mind, but it was not firm enough to challenge my whole life. I used to have an ordinary life, not an ordinary thought, until I heard the remarks of that psychologist on TV.

What was the result of this contradiction in my life? In fact, I did well in any field of interest. I really had ingenious ideas in my mind, but I don't know why I couldn't be serious in executing them. I jump-started energetically so that others were surprised, but it didn't last long. I either quit or reached my threshold and slowed down.

Until that moment, I didn't ask myself about the reason; now that I've got the answer, everything is alright. I was among the top ten in every aspect in a classroom of about 30 students. I played soccer so well that I was the second or the third choice of any captain but not good enough to be a captain. I was a sharp student who helped the weak ones in the classroom but not good enough to be a group leader. I rivaled to be the third or the fourth but not the first.

Meanwhile, in a small city like Rolla, they only talked about the first person. No one even cared about the second person, let alone the third or the fourth one! I have no idea if Rolla was a talented city or I was not good enough, at least to be seen in one of the sports, arts or even educational fields. Even my friends at school were starless fellows by whom I only spent my time. We were almost on the same level, but from every aspect, we were close to each other. The popular students at school never socialized with us.

I must say that in some fields, I ranked anywhere from second to fourth; however, the rest of guys were good only in one field. For example, the best basketball player of the class was among the students with low grades, and the best student, who was good at math, couldn't even jump rope.

It didn't make much difference to me because they were at least seen thoroughly even if they were weak in other fields. I was never seen in any field, though I was better than half of my classmates in all fields. It was my goal to become one of them. One of the stars!

The point about me is that inherently I didn't have any talent in any field to make me distinguished among others, but it was my enthusiasm and my endeavors that caused my progress. I had understood in advance that I didn't have the talent needed to make things easier for me. For instance, those who were good in sports didn't practice more than me. Top students, too, didn't study as much as I did. Altogether, things were easier for them. I had to fight to be able to stand at an acceptable level. I didn't struggle as much, as I might be called a hard-working person. I struggled more than many others, but it was unjust if they called me hard-working.

Christmas was just around the corner. Everyone was enjoying their holidays and waiting for Santa Claus to bring their gifts. It didn't make much difference to me. We were not a large family and didn't need to make a fuss. Christmas is a family celebration, so no one invited us, except a few of my father's friends. I had experienced my loneliness before, so it was not a new problem, but this time, there existed someone in my life for whom I should be Santa Claus to fulfill his wishes.

I still couldn't assimilate him to identify his needs as my own needs. Still, there was a long distance between Amir and Hossein that had to be covered. However, this time, I paid little attention to my surroundings. I was planning my goals, and I had to be seen.

I noted the fields I was good in on a piece of paper and started to check which one could be the best choice for me. As far as I remember, *he*, I mean Hossein, tried to persuade me do all things within my bounds. It meant that the fields I was good in were not too important. *He* didn't have a deep interest in any work. I myself, too, couldn't say what I liked more because I had never thought about it.

I wrote them down separately on a piece of paper and specified three topics for each: 1. "How good am I at …?" 2. "Conditions to reach the top", and 3. "My distance from the top student." Then I defined scores for each topic. The maximum score was 5. For example, I gave myself a 5 in chemistry, as I was good at it. For the second topic, I scored 1 because we did not have an equipped lab. For the last topic, I scored 2 because still there were four classmates better than me.

I assessed the rest of the fields of my interest. The result was not so desirable. In the end, I couldn't reach a specific field that I could focus my attention on. For instance, I was much better at chess, but the condition was not ripe for me to make a name for myself at school. In soccer, many of the students were better than me, and my chances of becoming famous were very slim. If I got a high score in one field, I scored low in another. Thus, my average score in all fields were almost the same.

Among those fields, performing in a theater was the most feasible one. Our school staff had an idea to set up a theater group and train some actors to compete at the State level. However, the case was not yet determined, and I couldn't count much on it. Anything could happen, so I decided not to abandon my plans.

I made up my mind to increase my efforts in all those fields, but as I had limited time and couldn't focus properly on my plans, I didn't want to strain myself. In the new year holidays, I made a clear plan so that I could manage and benefit for most of the remaining time.

I did more sports after new year holidays and the reopening of school. I increased my studying time and spent less time, even less than before, socializing around with friends.

A few weeks passed in this manner. I didn't talk much to my family, and my father didn't ask about my grades at school until it happened one night when they informed me about something.

While having his dinner, my father said, "Though I'm still displeased with you, and I've not forgotten your indecent manner a few weeks ago, I've to tell you about something. Your mother and I have decided to leave Rolla before the beginning of the new semester. I've reminded my colleagues to find me a job in one of the cities in California."

They expected me to be glad. All my plans would be ruined if we left there, and I couldn't be seen anymore. I was confused. I didn't know I had to be glad. So, I gave a very short answer, "It's OK."

My parents, bewildered by my indifference, asked me if the news did not make me happy. "At the moment, I am fixing my attention on my lessons. Final exams are near. Isn't it what you always asked from me?" I said.

My father who thought I was taunting him said, "do you ridicule me instead of thanking?"

I was not interested at all to continue the argument with my father, so I turned to him and said, "No, no. Not at all! Thanks a lot! It's all good news. I didn't mean it." I quickly left the table and went to my room to think what to do.

A BAD PROMISE

I thought a little and started to figure out my situation. I asked myself how sure it was that he could find the job—it could be a phony and bad promise. A little later, I thought that even if it was true, I wouldn't move away from my goal.

For sure, there were more facilities in bigger cities that provided better opportunities for me to exhibit. Though competing was more difficult there because of the higher number of students, I didn't need to be the top student to be at the center of attention. Of course, it didn't mean that I had to stop struggling and practicing, but I had to carry on to reach my goal under any situation.

On the one hand, I was ready and had motivation to start life in a new city; on the other, I could lose my motive because I would possibly find no one as a rival there. I know that I didn't have to be too sentimental, but you can't expect much from a 14-year-old boy. By the way, I had a static life in Rolla, and moving to a new city could be the biggest event in my life.

Nearly every night when I went to bed, I imagined myself in a new scene with new friends who, of course, neither one

36

heightened me, except when I saw myself lifted on the hands of others, or when the audience stood up while applauding me, and at the same moment I just started to count the people applauding me. It didn't matter at all, the way I was seen, so I imagined myself in all situations. Sometimes, I saw myself in a soccer field, on the stage of a theater, or receiving a school-prize for the top student, and in every situation, I delighted the same.

Nothing had changed in my life, but I had so much enthusiasm as if all my dreams had come true. In fact, I deserved to reach my goals. I already had spent my life in a black and white mode without any excitement, and it was time for me to give colors to my life.

In the interrogation room …

Amir says to Jill, "I don't know if others, too, might have a simple life with no ups and downs, but they had never thought about it, so they won't feel any shortages. I always preferred knowledge to ignorance, which was probably the reason why life has been more bitter for me. Life is too complicated.

It's not fair for man to be born once and die. Maybe if a human was born and grew up in a different situation, all their life was subject to change. Even in a more complicated way, if a human was born in exactly similar situation compared to his previous life, but bore different mentality, they could enjoy their life in a different way—just like me, who probably didn't need to have a different life. I just had to look at life in a different way so that I could enjoy life without feeling any loss. I believe that we humans don't reach the answer.

Maybe Einstein never reached the truth! Before putting forward the theory of relativity, he created the whole idea in his imagination, then looked for mathematical calculations to prove his imagination. Who knows if he reached the real truth; he could have only found an equation to prove his imaginations and present a practical theory in the real world.

Maybe the world is not what we see, but it is what we wish to see! Maybe, there was no hidden self in me, and the whole thing was just born in my imagination so I could give a meaning to my meaningless life. Maybe I never wished to be seen, and I was just looking for an excuse to prevent me from going insane!

Living once is not fair. In fact, a whole life will last long enough for man to know themselves, and it's where he reaches tranquility or insanity! Maybe, nothing will happen either, and they repeat the very first life in their second life, and they would try to eat more pizza pies than before! Is there really someone to have a clear answer?"

Jill, who was carefully taking notes of Amir's account statements, said, "If someone told you that you were going astray and you had to stop, would you really listen? I mean, you had reached all you wished for, so why did you have to stop?!"

Amir brought up his hands, put them on the desk, and said, "Exactly this is the point about my life! Maybe there's no absolute answer. Was there anyone who could judge whether I was right or wrong?"

"The law," Jill answered confidently. "The law is there for all the people to behave in a way that discipline is maintained in society."

Amir smiled sarcastically and said, "A law made by a few men, can't be a firm standard. From the viewpoint of a lawmaker, maybe something is bad, while it looks good to others. Anyway, I know where this debate leads to. They would say, "well, we have to have laws to be able to control the people and that a bad law is better than lawlessness," and they would repeat such words to the people so much that they would believe them. Repeat, repeat, and repeat! What values that got worthless by repetitions and vice versa—just like the so-called fashion. A way of thought or a way of clothing is repeated in society until the people follow it frantically. As I said, my only fault was that I wanted to be different even if it led to find me guilty."

Jill quickly said in a polite voice, "Of course, it's not a trial session here. I'm a reporter, and I don't intend to judge you, Mr. Shahri. Well, please carry on. How did you feel at that time? Amir, who earlier had almost a harsh tone, cooled down a little, and continued his journey…

In the story ….

All my efforts were to become good enough before the end of the semester so that I could draw attention of the others. I couldn't amuse others, so that I could attract them by flattering or blandishing. In fact, I tried it a few times, but I got very bad results, and when I faced the cold attitude of my fellows, I promised myself never to follow this way to attract attention of others. I was not made for this job at all.

I was neither seen so seriously that I could act with ease of mind to attract others so that they could explore me, nor did they look at me so casually that I could do silly things without being judged. I was stuck in between!

The problem didn't finish there, but it went further. I was stuck between him and myself! I mean, between Amir and Hossein! From the time I got to know him better, I couldn't have two different views in a single situation. For instance, when I saw Susan, I didn't know what reaction or emotion to have.

Amir asked me not to stop trying to get her back, but Hossein paid no attention at all and just wanted to defeat and belittle the guy who was drinking beer with her. It didn't mean that Hossein saw him as a rival and intended to attain his goal 'Susan' by leaving him behind. Rather, *he* just didn't want to have any excuse for not reaching his goal. It was all right for him to think that *he* would obtain anything *he* wished for. He didn't have the thirst to obtain it; he just wanted to prove to me from within that he was the best one.

When I saw Susan at school, I had two completely different feelings at the same time. It was as though I was having a frozen ice-cream and drinking a hot coffee! I felt like being dragged from two opposing sides, and in the middle of all this my soul was suffering because *he* didn't know exactly what feeling it should have.

Frankly, it was not long before I had become aware of a new being within me, but my mind was not accustomed to having a new roommate! Of course, I was more worried about a bigger problem. My friends had pointed out to me that I had changed a little. On the one hand, I just wanted to deny that fact; on the other, *he* had become tired of being hidden and wished to introduce himself to the new world.

At that moment, I had to try not to listen to him and just speak my mind. It was not a simple thing, because he used to repeat his words in my mind, and I had to transfer my own words from my mind to my tongue. It is as though you are busy talking to someone while another individual begins whispering in your ear, and you have to concentrate on your words in a way your interlocutor doesn't understand!

Things were getting a little complex. I felt a kind of disorder in my mind, but I was not too tired to give up everything and ignore him. I thought that after a while, we both would harmonize, and the existing personality disorder would disappear. I couldn't ask anyone what to do, because I was alone from the beginning, and I had to finish the road trip alone. I had no desire to do my daily routines, but I was too eager to do my intensive trainings to improve my skills. I was like a student who puts his or her school lessons aside to be able to study for Olympiad contests and exceptional talents tests.

It was not long before the end of the semester, and I couldn't feel the impact of my trainings and studies during that short time. Whenever I felt under pressure from my trainings and studies, my mind gave me promise that I wouldn't keep staying in Rolla and probably living in a place would be better and easier.

I had no idea why I was so optimistic. It caused me to stop training when I reached the difficult part of it because part of my inner self didn't believe in excessive pressure when I could achieve without it. I considered it as a good omen, but there was no guarantee because for a long time, I was looking for a good happening.

During that time, nothing special had happened in my life. Sometimes, when I faced some ordinary things, the newly explored part within me tried to introduce a new vision towards that thing. My daily schedule had slightly become more intense and I was not looking for a miracle!

I just imagined myself in the new academic year in a new place and new people, and it was possibly the reason why my life and daily routine seemed more faded. I always had a high power of imagination, but it was not as if I would spend all my life living fantasies.

The semester was over, and summer holidays started with our school grades not so unexpected. The summer had no attraction to me. I've no idea why I didn't doubt about it. I was sure good news was on the way. One of the things I had to do was remove the distance between *he* and I. I felt like watching horror movies as if a ghost or an unknown being had captured me from outside, and I was not truly myself either.

41

I thought about it several times and blamed myself for approaching so easily with it. Probably any other person who faced with that phenomenon would have tried to oust the unknown personality from within himself and start to explore it. Such people are insane. I'm sure almost no-one else could have solved the problem the way I did.

After thinking on that issue for a while, I had a feeling that because others didn't have the capacity to accept it as a reality and tried to deny it, they would probably never reach the point where they wanted to explore it. Before something is approved, it should be wanted.

Men usually deny everything that is unknown and disrupts their daily routine because they are scared of accepting terrible incidents but I was looking for it. I was always looking for the unknown and truth that hardly anyone would have accepted. I just wanted to believe that there is a mystery behind this simple life and a complicated formula behind every simple equation.

In summer, when everybody is looking for recreation and relaxing their brains after months of exploiting it, I had been challenged by my thoughts. After all, I had learned how to think, and I had understood that thinking is not just repeating what we already have learned.

Thinking is a way to reach to the unknown. So, maybe there has never been a mere truth from the beginning. Maybe the truth is what we wish to believe in! Maybe the others could never reach what I reached because they didn't want to believe. Maybe the truth for them is to deny and for me to confirm!

Basically, cases about personality and metaphysics are not observable are neither confirmable nor deniable. The reasons which are usually introduced are undecided and unprovable and are only used to justify the viewpoint of some people. Maybe, Satan exists for the one who believes in him, and it is just a product of mind for the one who doesn't believe. As the devil can't be seen or be talked to, one can't say if he exists or not. Thus, maybe there existed no *he* from the beginning, and it was only me who tried to disrupt my daily routine to have a refreshing change and forget my colorless and monotonous life.

After all those challenging thoughts I had every day and night, it was time to decide. I set to compare myself before finding him with myself after to see if it was worth it to change the whole route of my life. I found out that previously, my whole life was summarized in musts and must-nots that others used to define for me.

I had no reason to revolt. Even if I was looking for success, it should be limited in a framework that others had defined for me. The others, the others, and the others. Others always defined limits for me. Even I was not free in my wishes, just like a vast garden surrounded by fences.

At the first glance, man doesn't feel like being a prisoner and thinks that he is experiencing freedom in all senses. Everything is already prepared in his vast garden—every amusement and every kind of fruit. There are so many amusing things that man finds no time to think about outside.

The point here is that if someone intends to exit the garden, are they allowed to? It doesn't matter how fun it is inside the garden or if all the needs of man are met. It's a jail, though beautiful and charming. My life, too, was like that garden, where everything was already prepared, and I had the right to choose between every tree and every fruits, but only I didn't have the permission to exit.

I thought a little and saw that I had been in the garden enough to try many of the fruits! What keeps man in the garden is his greed and desire to try bigger fruits with new flavors. To realize their wishes, people do their utmost to reach the scarce fruits in the garden. So, it couldn't be a real wish when that need and greed is moved by the wishes of others. Even if, for instance, I could gain access to a scarce fruit and taste its flavor, it was just a fruit of the same garden!

I had a feeling that I had strolled enough in that garden. Now it was the time to find the truth beyond the walls of the garden, where I possibly could find my real self, not the self that others had made for me! I had made nothing to fear losing. Beyond the wall, I had found something in myself that was made before, and it was the best part of it.

That was not me who inculcated myself to pursue superiority and being seen. The idea was given to me even before I start thinking about it. It was as if I faced an intelligent being. Maybe, I incurred loss, but as I said, I would lose nothing special.

I made my decision after a few weeks of continuous thinking and comparing things. I had to allow *him* to enter me. We had to unite so that I would find out how far that dark part would take me. After having made my decision, I had to think out how to dissolve him in me so that no trace of him was found outside me! This way, if someone asked me a question, two answers wouldn't pop into my mind, and I wouldn't have to try one of them! There shouldn't remain a trace so that no one can detect the change in me.

Fortunately, it was summer, and compared with school days when we used to see each other, I had a faded relationship with my fellows. Maybe they would say that Amir had changed a little. Well, it's natural. I hit puberty, a reason for others not to become suspicious of me. I shouldn't feel him in me, either. *He* had to become me, and I had to become him—two souls in a single body. I had to completely dissolve him within my personality. In the meantime, I had to continue my trainings for the upcoming semester and for a new school and new place.

It was as if I had fully trusted in him and enjoyed the trip as far as the road went on. The way to dissolve him and unite him with my personality was not so difficult and just needed some more trainings. Every morning when I woke up, soon after I received his first message, I did what he ordered, and at the same time, I kept it in my mind.

The next day, before I got into the mood for anything, I did things myself. If it happened that I was inclined to do more things, I understood that I should do something else. Day by day, I got to know him more. By repeating what *he* ordered me to do the days before, I resembled him more. I repeated so much that it turned into a habit for me, and before my brain received any message, I did it.

Of course, it was not that easy. In the beginning, for instance, I noticed that *he* didn't let me sleep at night by filling my mind with irrelevant issues. That way, I understood I had done something wrong that *he* didn't let me finish my night, but as that damned *'he'* didn't talk, I couldn't realize what things I had forgotten to do. It was the point that had made me a little dispirited. It strengthened a sense in me to think that all these are no more than a story made up in my mind.

Why, sometimes, should *he* talk to me in detail about what to say and what to do, like the days I played soccer—when *he* took my full control in such a way that I was just an onlooker? Sometimes, *he* left me all alone; I didn't know what I had to do. However, I had promised myself not to throw a monkey wrench into my own wheel even if the idea seemed totally stupid.

In a few days I tried a few different things, like reading novels before sleeping, watching TV, staring at the sky, etc. One night, when I already had made my room tidy and in order, as soon as I put my head on the pillow, I fell into a deep sleep. The next morning I woke up, I realized that last night, I had done the same thing *he* asked of me and remembered that the difference between last night and the nights before was that my room was organized!

Thereafter, I tried to be neat and regular in everything like putting my clothes and everything in order. That point helped me much, because sometimes, when I felt that *he* wanted to tell me something, but I couldn't establish a full relationship with him, the problem disappeared as soon as I was neat and organized. After a while, when I felt I knew him enough, I told myself that sooner or later, I was going to face people.

Thereafter, I went out of my room and spent more time with my friends and family. That socialization was limited to the extent that I could assess his interaction with others. My fellows were surprised to see how I had abandoned my solitude and returned to society. However, I gained good experiences in that regard. For instance, my relationship, or better to say, *his* relationship with my father was such that if *he* was supported or encouraged by father, *he* warmly welcomed the family, but when there was an argument, his reaction was so aggressive.

In the meantime, I ensured the red lines were not stepped over. As my father had promised us to move to another city, which was great news, I didn't want to lose the chance or do something that made him change his mind. *He* had the same approach with my friends. If someone showed disrespect or was not polite with him, *he* showed a harsh reaction the way I do.

Before that, maybe I had heard much worse than these things, but I didn't take it seriously and used to think that it was just a friendly banter. On the other hand, *he* understood others more than me. So, others preferred to speak with him or better to say me with his version. Though *he* was colder and less affectionate, *he* was more of a justice seeker than me.

Sometimes, he reminded me to be thoughtful when I neglected

many important things. For instance, at the birthday party of a neighbor, when a friend of mine received a small portion of the cake, *he* asked me to give my piece of cake to the guy. It was not an important thing, and my friend even told me it didn't matter at all and didn't accept my offer. I knew it was because of *his* justice seeking, not his kindness.

He was sensitive about my personality and even about my handwriting! I didn't have good handwriting. When I took the pen in my hand and started to write something down, *he* got upset as if someone was screaming in my mind, and so I had to write more attentively. After a while, when I compared my previous handwriting with my new one, I could hardly believe that the two were my own. It was as if two different persons had written them.

He had a great interest to file everything. Every now and then *he* put thoughts in me, making me refer to the things I already had collected in order to remember them. *He* hated digression, unlike me—I spent much time on things that didn't have impact on my life. *He* always asked me to take a note when I saw a movie, read a book, or talked about ordinary things with my friends. I had become a movie critic!

He was more isolated than me. *He* unwillingly attended a gathering. If *he* owned my feet, *he* would have never let me join a gathering unless I shined there. Gradually, I found out that *he* didn't enjoy accompanying others, but *he* was fond of standing higher than them. *He* welcomed it if there was a challenge like playing football with my friends. I always checked to see if a player better than me took part in the play, and if so, stress filled my whole body.

Since I let him enter my nerves, my stress had greatly decreased because *he* was so enthusiastic that *he* didn't let stress and fear approach me. His courage was the most attractive part of his personality; I needed it more than anything. That way, I could free myself from anxiety and authorize him to gain control of

47

my mind when I was surrounded by difficult situations.

I entrusted to him whatever I wanted and didn't have the courage to gain. Every day, I got a step closer to *Hossein*, but I kept my original self, Amir. After about a month and a half, I had nearly become Amirhossein! By getting closer to the end of the summer holidays, I got more excited to face the new challenge ahead. When I was able to unite with him to an acceptable extent, I began concentrating more on my trainings.

I was turned into a disciplined person and had a real feeling that I was not so far from a future where I would become a successful individual. My whole vacation passed in trial and error by examining my new personality. The result was unexpectedly good. Without waiting to receive any sign from him, I was able to speak what *he* wished to say and do what *he* asked me for. Every time after I spoke or acted, *he* didn't tickle my mind to get in touch; I got to know that my words or deeds were the same as *he* wanted.

The last days I had become so much like him that nearly I didn't feel his presence. I couldn't exactly say if *he* had gained full control of my mind. I couldn't recognize his presence or absence. Anyway, the feeling of duality was no longer there, and I was just myself—or I was us!

Mostly, I talked to my family and nearly always raised the issue of our move and asked my father about our new place of residence. My father looked a little weird. He didn't give a direct answer, as if he hid something from me. I thought that because he had got used to our living place—and was about to change his job and dwelling place for the sake of me—he would be a little upset. I understood him and didn't intend to make him annoyed, but occasionally, I lost my control and raised the issue again.

Only a few weeks were left until the beginning of the new semester, and I had not enrolled for my new school. I saw my parents, who talked to each other late at night, make eye contact at dinner table, but I paid no attention at all.

Through the whole summer, I was busy self-training. I anxiously waited and thought only about that moment. A few days passed in that manner, and I began to fear that I had a disease and that my parents didn't want to inform me. One night when we were sitting at a quiet dinner table, I decided to break the silence of my parents and ask them frankly if they were hiding something from me. My father intended to talk, but we stayed silent by looking at each other and waiting for the other one to start talking.

My father and I stared at each other for a few seconds. I understood from his eyes that I had to wait to hear bad news. "Did you want to say something?" he said.

After looking at my parents for a few seconds, I said, "I wanted to ask the same thing you are about to say!"

"How did you know what I intended to say?" My father asked.

I wanted to continue the argument, but in the meantime, as I was *him* more than myself, I replied in *his* manner, "Just say it without any turning aside!"

I felt that my parents were looking for a chance to break the heavy atmosphere. They were disappointedly looking at my grim and determined face. My father, who was almost astonished, said, "Your mother and I have decided to talk to you about something. It's been a while since your behavior has changed, and you're no longer like before."

I, who had become certain they were hiding something from me and were looking for a proper chance, said in an impassive tone, "Please say. No need for any preparations!"

My father quickly said, "Like right now. Your way of talking. We exactly wanted to talk about it. If you have any problems with your friends, that's no reason for you to be edgy and bad-tempered at home."

I quickly cleaned my lips with a napkin, drew my chair back and got ready to leave the table, but my father angrily shouted, "Sit down!"

The atmosphere of our house was no more a family one. It was just like an interrogation room. My whole body was filled with anger. I stood and stared at my father. He reacted in a stark voice: "You leave the dinner table when I allow you!"

We were both like a fire ablaze. I never had such an experience of quarrel or dispute. I didn't know what to do. No! Maybe I knew it. I mean I didn't know, but *he* knew it. I always used to run away from tension and had no particular experience in those situations, but *he* always looked for excitement and tensions at any moment.

I remembered the second thing *he* asked me was jumping out of my room's window even though I never thought about it. My hands started to shiver. I had chocked a little with anger. My eyes had turned red. My breath was coming in gasps in such a way everyone could hear. I gently squeezed my fist.

I dared say that it was not me but him. Although I had exercised much to become like him, this time, it was something different. I did never have an experience of such aggression. Of course, it was not so bad; I took it as a new lesson to get a better relationship with *him*.

My father continued, "From now on, as long as you stay here, you will act according to the rules of this house." I stretched out my hand to the glass of water on the table that had water, took it to the right side, and lifted it up to my shoulders.

All the while, my mother kept silent and looked. She didn't know what to do or say. At last, she broke her silence and called my name. My father stared at me and waited to see what

I wanted to do. Even I waited to see what *he* would finally do.

Suddenly, I unintentionally said, "Shall I take your permission for this, too?" Just before my father opened his mouth to ask "permission for what", I threw the glass of water on the floor! My mother screamed. The sound of the glass breaking was much louder than I expected. Maybe it was because of the prevailing silence in the room. Pieces of the broken glass were thrown all over the hall.

My father stood up quickly, came to me, and grasped my collar with both his hands. My mother tried to split us. My father had lost his temper but somehow controlled himself and released his right hand so he could slap my face. I distanced myself from him, but he caught me by the collar with his left hand, lifted his right hand, and shouted angrily.

Before that time, he had never beaten me. His face was red with anger. He bit his lip and stared at me. I was not watching an eye-catching scene, of course, but I felt at ease. *His* presence in my mind caused my feelings to fade.

The feeling I had at that moment was like one in which I was sitting in a movie theatre and watching an action movie, but I was not eating popcorn! My mother screamed, and my father shouted. His right hand was shivering in the air and ready to slap on my face. We were right under the lights in the hall, and I could feel the shadow of his hand over my face.

I was dangling in the air while sweat covered my whole body. A shadow on my face had created an almost pleasant feeling, and I was standing in an interesting position. I impulsively remembered a scene from the movie 'Jaws' where people along the seashore were stretching on their lounge chairs and busy sunbathing. They seemed to be dangling in the air and used parasol umbrellas to get rid of the sunlight.

I had no idea why a scene from a movie came into my mind in

such a sensitive situation. First, I thought that because of Hossein, I hadn't become sentimental; the possible reason behind my impulsive remembering of a scene from a movie was the cause of the calm within me. I knew that *he* sometimes made me think about things not agreeable with the situation I was in. Maybe it was one of those occasions. Later, I thought that I remembered it because I stood in a situation almost the scene in that movie.

Maybe I was unifying my memories with my mind, but if it was so, it didn't look logical at all. All those thoughts jumped into my mind in a matter of a second as if the time stood still so I could think with ease in that peculiar situation. I abandoned my thoughts, regained my consciousness, and the first image I saw was the irritated face of my father with his hand getting closer to me.

I vaguely heard my father's shouts and my mother's screams, just like a person that had a explode close to his ear and the blast wave. I fully came back to myself when my father changed his mind about beating me, but he caught me by my collar with both his hands and threw me to a corner of the hall with all his power and a loud roar.

Fortunately, my back hit the legs of the sofa, which protected my head from suffering harm. I leaned my back against the sofa and stretched my feet on the floor. I wondered if all this was a dream or a reality. My mother went to my father to see if he was all right. My father, unable to stand on his feet, threw himself on the dinner table and was gasping for breath like he was suffering a heart attack. I felt like a toy thrown to a corner of a room and void of any feeling to make a move or change his position. I was staring at a corner; I did not think or speak.

My mother gave a glass of water to my father and asked him to talk to her about his health. I didn't think about my father at all. Right at that moment, the same scene of the beach in the movie 'Jaws' leaped into my mind once more. I myself had no role in remembering that scene. Why should that movie come back to my mind? I was no more in a similar situation, either. So, why? There should be another reason.

A little while after the calm and pleasure resulting from watching the seashore returned, a shark attacked the children swimming in the sea, turning the joy and pleasure into a nightmare. I was in a similar situation, dangling in the air under the shadow of my father's hand and being thrown at a corner. Again, I couldn't convince myself that it was the reason why I remembered that peculiar scene.

In the meantime, I saw my father—who had gotten better— and could stand on his feet. He drank some water; his heartbeat became somewhat regular, and in a cold but calm tone said, "I can't stand your disrespects anymore. I must change my parenting. This way, you have no place at this house. By the way, we will not be moving. I didn't beat you this time, but if you continue such behavior, you'll surely regret it. Now, stand up and collect the pieces of glass."

I did not wish it was a dream because of what happened between my father and I but because of the very last news. It was so bad I couldn't take it in. In a moment, the whole world became dark to my eyes. It was as if someone was whistling in my ears. My previous negative feelings had come back to me. It made me feel severely disappointed and depressed. All the things I had dreamed of were turned into a null. All my thoughts and imaginations throughout the day and night were wasted. The very thing my parents intended to say, but hid from me, was just this.

At that moment, I fully understood their weird attitude during the past weeks. They felt embarrassed to tell me the truth, because they saw how frantically I was wishing for it. All that time, I was happy and motivated for an illusory hope. There was not any bidding goodbye with friends, neighbors, school, or my city, either. I had to live the same life I didn't like.

Everything was swirling around my head. I didn't feel well at all. The scene of the movie 'Jaws' appeared in my mind again. Until then, 'Jaws' was one of favorite movies, but a feeling of hatred about it was growing in me. At that moment, of course, everything that appeared in front of my eyes seemed hateful to me. Unintentionally, I started to whisper words I didn't know the meanings of. My mother was trying to soothe me by saying that maybe I didn't feel well, and that was why I lost my control at that moment; my father was trying to defend himself, so my mother tried to claim that I was still guilty.

My parents were busy talking about me when my whispering drew their attention. They turned toward me and focused to understand what I said, and I did the same! That time, I had a feeling that it was *he* who was talking without my permission and sharing my thoughts.

The scene from 'Jaws' appeared in my mind again. I could feel his presence from the eyes of the child who was attacked by the shark at the seashore and from the big bubbles going up to the surface of water. For a moment, I looked at my parents, and for the other moment, I saw the shark through the eyes of that child. I realized that my voice had got clearer after seeing the shark that quickly got closer to the child's feet. My father, who was not in the mood at all, said in an imperative tone, "Speak louder so that I can hear you."

My voice steadily got louder—I could understand what I was saying. I repeated to myself, "It was not supposed from the beginning that you beat me. I was supposed to beat myself!" What I repeated seemed nonsense. The scene of the shark attacking the child marched twice in front of my eyes. Finally, after a few different guesses, I could find out the relationship between my present situation and that scene from the movie. The scene came to me because I was in a motionless position, like the people resting at the shore, and after being thrown to a corner by my father, I exited that peaceful situation like the people who frantically tried to escape from the shark.

It was not my father who could ruin everything by throwing me aside or even slapping on my face and playing the so-called role of the shark. I was the shark who attacked the child and ruined everything! The child who was attacked by the shark was me, too!. Even the people sunbathing near the seashore were me! I was everyone! The whole movie was me!

It was not my father who attacked me, but I was the one who made him attack me. I finally understood what *he* wanted to show me through all that time. It doesn't matter who does what, but it is important that who's behind it all. It was me who composed the scenario that way, and that was why I unintentionally repeated, "It was not supposed from the beginning that you beat me. I was supposed to beat myself!"

I had to beat myself, because I wanted to. I turned my head to the flowerpot on the table near the chair I was leaning against. While continuously repeating that sentence, I stretched my hand, took that flowerpot, and cast down my head. Before my parents showed any reaction, I hit my head with the flowerpot. It caused a severe pain. I kept hitting my head with the pot while thinking about both the bad news my father gave and the shark biting the child's feet.

Thinking about the bad news eased my pain. My parents hurried toward me and pulled the pot out of my hand. I don't remember anything else. Maybe, it didn't matter for me to remember.

THE TALL MAN

It was so distressing for me to think that through all that time, I was struggling in vain. Maybe I had been daydreaming too much. *His* presence meant nothing to me anymore. All over, Hossein was a Hollywood dream and no more. I just had lost my summer to a phantom dream and a possibly self-made and imaginary personality.

From the next day on, I was not him. I was a depressed and downhearted Amir. I neither went out or talked to anybody. My parents tried to explain to me that they had made all their efforts to move from Rolla, but my father had failed to find a proper job in another city. I even didn't let them get close to me.

His presence was dangerous. My insanity had risen to the extreme, and I did things that were not brave but stupid. I was displeased with myself. I was deceived by my imagination and thought I could give birth to a superman out of my inner self. *He* had no place in my mind anymore, but his trace had already been stabilized in my personality.

Yet, I wished to be the best. I couldn't ignore it because I really wanted it and was looking for a pretext to have it. I had lost all my self-confidence. I, who granted peace to others through my conversations and keeping company with them, needed, more than anyone, to confide with others.

I didn't have the boldness he gave me anymore. I had returned to my old personality of a loser, but I didn't do irrational things anymore. I didn't have any reason to keep him with me. I was out of the frying pan and into the fire! I wondered if I had to return to my former lifestyle or continue *his* way. My enthusiasm for the beginning of the school year was reversed. Before I knew that we were going to stay in Rolla, I counted the days of the summer to finish and start a new life in a new place. After it was decided that we wouldn't go anywhere, I wished time would stop so that I didn't have to meet the same school, the same faces, and the same days again.

Before Hossein started to form in me, I didn't have much problem with my living place. After *he* instigated my father through my tongue and made him promise to move to another city, I was such that I only wished to get rid of that city, its people, and its ordinary, boring days. I just looked for salvation in any place out of Rolla. *He* was gone, but I was not willing to continue a life in that style. The reason was so clear. What Hossein had brought me as a souvenir was nothing but ambition and superiority.

Considering my greed for honor, Rolla couldn't be a proper answer. I was afraid of being ignored. As I couldn't overtake the speed of light and slow down the time, I got closer, day by day, wittingly or unwittingly, to the beginning of school.

Just two weeks were left to the beginning of the new semester. I had become like the insane and used to think and walk steadily in my room. I reviewed all possible options to see if still there remained any way for me to bring about a name for myself at school. At night, I used to think for hours in my bed, and fell asleep near dawn.

Until then, I didn't have the chance to see the dawn. The window of my room faced the north, and so I couldn't see the dawn. I had heard much about it and always wished to see it. It's always the same when something is within your access that you are in no hurry to get, but as soon as it becomes unavailable, you leave no stone unturned!

I found myself in a state of psychosis and thought if I didn't help myself, I would die before the beginning of school. As I had lost all my self-confidence, I started to put forward childish hypotheses in order to give hope to myself.

I thought to myself that I had gained some skills both with and without his help. I spent my summer exercising my talents. Of course, I didn't have such severe trainings, but I had tried to adapt myself to Hossein. Maybe the very no such hard trainings had made me distinguished from others, and I didn't know it! Maybe those who were superior to me in every field had either moved to a new place or changed their school. Maybe they were not as good as before! Who knows? Anything could have happened, and as long as I didn't go to school, I wouldn't have realized it.

I felt a little better, but I was still somewhat fearful. Sometimes, I cursed at him because *he* had left me; I was still occupied with him, and *he* had caused my personality to change.

Finally, after all those happenings in summer, the schools opened, and I went to school. In the first day of school, my first hope faded when I saw my rivals there. Worse than that were the new faces who could possibly be my new rivals and better than me.

I was so careful to see if they were active in the same fields as me. I had become like a child who once burned his hands while playing with fire and feared any radiant object thereafter. Every moment, I was waiting to see if anyone would show their arts to attract other's attention. I even had become sensitive to the taunts my classmates said and made others laugh.

I had a feeling that all attention should be on me, and I shouldn't lag behind anyone in anything. I had become even more timid than my old personality. After about two weeks, my hopes gradually faded away when I realized that they were better than me. Indeed, my distance with other students had become smaller considering my light but steady trainings in summer.

Nevertheless, I had not made a step forward, and nobody had formed a guard of honor for me because of my efforts to reduce my rank with others. I was not even the second one in any of the fields. I could say that all my hopes had faded away. I had no reason to be happy. I was a loser to myself and others.

Was it my fault that I always had to wait for good news? Maybe I expected more than my capacity. Anyway, it didn't matter. I could not think ordinarily so that I didn't have to suffer or be good enough to enjoy being the best person. I thought to myself that even if I could have heavy and centralized trainings throughout the summer in just one field, it was no use because I had a long distance with the first person.

School and home were hell to me. I had no place to take refuge in. My only break was the time I used to walk home from school. As I didn't have the patience for anybody, I preferred to walk alone. Our house was on fox creek road, about two miles from Rolla high school and about five minutes away when driving.

Like the year before, my close friends at school were Cody, Jacob, and Henry. We used to spend our break time and lunch time together. We would not die for each other, but we attentively listened to each other.

I felt so absurd from within that I managed to reduce my distance with my friends more than before. I saw others with their ordinary and vulgar beliefs as a hurdle in my way of self-recognition and perfection, but I had to spend more time with them and even laugh at their insipid jokes so that I would feel I was completely accepted by them.

As I couldn't have the experience of being important in a bigger scale like school, it occurred in my mind that I could maybe be at the center of attention of my friends. The point was that they had accepted me as their friend, not as their boss, so they didn't show any willingness to my suggestions. They just wanted to do what others did.

I failed to set up something like a group so that I could be the leader or the so-called first person. After I got disappointed by that idea, I thought to myself that if I returned to my previous life, the feeling of attracting the attention of others within me would fade away more than before. Soon, I understood that I was wrong in my opinion. I wouldn't return to my previous situation.

The time I walked home from school was the best part of my life. There was a gap between the two bitter ends of my life. I liked it the way I never got to school on my way from home, and not to get home on my way back from school. I wished to be always on the way, as nothing waited for me at home or school.

As I said before, once you get wise, it's impossible to become ignorant. I had realized the vanity of daily routine, but after his leaving me, I didn't dare swim upstream. I had a cold relationship with my family. Most of the times, I used to have my dinner alone. Mostly, I had my lunch alone not because I wanted to be alone but because my mother had found a few friends with whom she went out shopping with.

I had the spare key to the house so I wouldn't be locked out when there was no one home. It didn't matter to me at all because except in necessary cases, I didn't spend my time with family. In the meantime, I had found a bicycle repair job. The owner of the repair shop had given me a bike to go to school, but I preferred to walk so that it took longer to get to school.

One day, I was returning home alone. Like every day, I was busy reviewing the past months happenings in my mind while spinning the key ring on my pointer finger out of habit. I accidentally spun the key ring so quickly that it slipped from my finger, and in accordance to Murphy's law, it was thrown to the farthest place around! I was so busy thinking that I didn't realize it, but after a few steps, I happened to see my finger without the key ring on it.

I returned quickly but failed to find it. The ring was grey, and it was a bit difficult to distinguish it from the color of the sidewalk's cobblestones. I was so mentally exhausted that the smallest problems seemed oversized to me. Losing the key ring was not the end of the world, but for me, it was so unnerving.

As I was hopelessly looking for the key, a tall man appeared from where I didn't know. He had a bony face and wore a chevron mustache. His western hat, dark brown vest, light blue shirt, and jeans with a snakeskin belt exhibited a slightly different appearance compared with the ordinary people of Rolla.

I don't know why, but there was a charisma in his face that made me astounded as if I had seen the president from near. I was really amazed, and I didn't know why. Maybe I was defeated so much that I needed to admire someone. He came toward me, and while smiling, he gave me the keys and said, "I think these are for you, young man." I, who could not talk properly, replied with a simple thank you and just gazed at him. He, too, simply passed by and continued his way.

He had a different style and a different approach, but I've no

61

idea why he amazed me. Frankly, it was long since someone
had helped me. Everything that happened was routine. I lived
in a lifeless city, and no one loved me. Maybe my parents
tolerated me and held my responsibility as their duty. It was as
if they were on a mission to take care of me, not because they
really loved me from the heart.

It made no difference for our teachers whether we enjoyed our
lessons. It was just because teaching was their job. My friends,
too, made friends with me, because a set of things like greeting
and talking to each other were means of friendship. I had a
feeling that if those things were not a must and not expected in
friendship, maybe they didn't listen to me, either. Nevertheless,
that man gave me the keys, which he had no duty or
responsibility of doing.

By all of this, I mean that no one lived with a sense of purpose.
I needed someone to understand me more than any time.
However, that day passed, and I spent days without looking for
anything.

A few days later, I saw that man in a supermarket was
shopping with the very same smile on his face. I had not seen
him in the city before. Maybe he was a newcomer. Later, I saw
him several times with his special way of looking and walking
that expressed his personality. I don't know why, but every
time after I saw him, I got the feeling as if I had been waiting
for him so long.

Among all those colorless, meaningless, and repeated days,
seeing him was the only good thing happening for me.
Another time when I saw him, I was influenced by him more
than before. While busy doing a classroom-based research
paper, I saw him sitting on a bench and smoking a cigarette in
Ber Juan Park. Till then, I had not enjoyed seeing someone
smoke a cigarette. With that usual hat on his head and a
cigarette on his lips, he was looking at nature.

I saw such calm look on his face that I got the feeling that nothing could bring him down. I could easily feel that he has sovereignty and full control of his life. I felt a little envious. It was a long time I wished to have a feeling of spiritual tranquility. As we had once met before, I tried not to show myself and watch him from behind a tree.

The fire of his cigarette had not reached the filter when he threw it down in front of his foot, but apparently, he forgot to put his leg on it. He fixed his hat a little, stood up, and started to walk at a regular pace. At that moment, I just wished I were him. Immediately after he distanced from the bench, I went and sat on it just like he was sitting, picked up his cigarette butt off the ground, and put it on my lips. I tried to look around and smoke the cigarette just the way he did.

I only could puff on the cigarette butt once or twice, but I coughed and got hurt as if it was the first time I smoked. I got a sense that he owned all I needed to gain inner satisfaction and that he was the only one who could help me enjoy whatever I had. I had in mind to ask him whether his calm and charisma were because he had gained whatever he wished for, or because he had paid no attention to this life and its belongings so that he would not be disturbed because of what he didn't have.

What could really be his goal in life that he could live so peacefully in this small city, as if the whole world was there? Maybe his life was not as I sensed, and it was just my impression. Maybe he had got lots of problems in his private life, and I didn't know about it. Whatever it was, I could say it inspired a good feeling in me to think that he thought the way as I did and had the same sensations as I had.

I decided to appear in front of him just unexpectedly as he did and ask my questions. On the one hand, my questions seemed to be weird, and on the other, we didn't know each other— maybe he would feel I intended to tease him. I had to practice in order to convince him that my questions were serious and that I really wished to have his advice. Because of our age difference, I had to be cautious and practice in advance the words I intended to tell him, as it would be difficult to believe that those words were spoken by a person my age!

As I did not have the courage as before, I always feared not to be able to build a relationship with others, especially with a man much older than me, and it made me stressed. To lift my spirit, I used to listen to Queen - We Will Rock You. I have no idea, but maybe because that tall man's face resembled Freddie Mercury; I had got more interested in the band Queen whose mustaches really made them even more like him.

Every day, I prepared a text for talking to the tall man and used to practice it a lot, and at night, I gathered that text was not enough. I had arranged as many different scenarios as how to approach the man, that I got confused. Every day on my way back home from school, I practiced in such a way that if someone saw me talking with myself, they probably would think I had gone insane.

For a week or two, I continued to practice facing the tall man. I imagined him, say, appearing from behind a tree or an alley and abruptly started talking to him.

On my way home, I was passing the Buehler-Breuer park at the beginning of the alley where our house located, so I decided to imagine him there, too. I got closer to the trees of the park as if he was talking to me from behind the them. It was more like an acting class, and I was practicing my role. sometimes It caused me to practice playing the role and not to think at all where I was or if anyone was watching, as it had become something normal to me. As soon as I would find an interesting location, I practiced my dialogues there.

The next day we had chemistry class, the teacher finished his chalk and left the class for a short time to take some chalk.

Cody, who was sitting next to me asked me who I was talking to in the park the day before. I, who didn't remember the day before, said indifferently, "No one! I was not talking to anyone in the park yesterday."

I had not finished talking, and Jacob and Henry, who were sitting the row behind us, said in a firm and stubborn voice, "Yeah! We saw with our own eyes that you were talking with someone. Tell me, who was it who tried to hide himself?" I reviewed the whole day before to see if I was in the park, but I didn't remember anything. "I told you: No one! I was home the whole day," I replied.

Jacob cut in, "No, I mean on your way back home. Now I understand why when the school finishes, you don't accompany us and go back home alone. Tell me! Tell me! Why should a guy talk to you covertly from behind the trees?" They demanded me so excitedly and in enthusiasm that I suppose they would have strangled me if I hadn't replied to their question.

But the truth is that I didn't remember at all if I talked to anybody... oh! Wait a minute! They had seen me in Breuer park while I was practicing my dialogue with the tall man, but because they were passing by the side alley, they mistook me talking with myself.

As soon as I realized and opened my mouth to say that it was just me who was practicing an imaginary dialogue, the teacher came back to the class and carried on with the lesson. So, I told them I would explain it after the class. About twenty minutes were left to the end of the class, and the whole time, I was thinking what to say after the class. It was good that the teacher came back on time, and I couldn't answer. Because if he had come later, the story would be different.

Possibly, they would think that I had gone insane. That way, I would lose my face and maybe the only friends I had would

distance themselves from me, fearing that I had lost my mental
health. I was thinking about those things when all of a sudden,
a thought occurred to me and gave me goosebumps.

All the time, I had tried to draw the attention of others so that
I could be seen, and despite all my efforts, I didn't succeed.
This time, however, it was different. My friends had come to
me and were anxiously waiting for me to talk to them. It's true
that their enthusiasm was not for the sake of me, but it was
because they tried to know the guy who had a secret
relationship with me. Thus, I took it easy and was so happy
because of the attention being paid to me that I just wished the
time would stop so that I could look at their faces who were
eagerly staring at me.

It was a golden chance I couldn't lose. None of them should
have understood that no guy was behind the scene, otherwise I
would have no more attraction for my friends. But, twenty
minutes' time was not enough for me to compose a convincing
story. I was drenched in sweat. Unlike all other chemistry
classes that we had before, the time passed so quickly. When
the class finished, before I put my things inside my schoolbag,
they gathered around me in a matter of a seconds. They
wanted to hear just a clear answer: Who was the guy talking to
me from behind the trees?

Again, I refused to speak. I finally answered in a voice that was
intentionally hiding something from them. The more I denied,
the more they implored, and it was the most delightful feeling
possible for me. "We'll talk about it later. I have to go!" I said
confidently.

I quickly left the classroom and headed home. I changed my
clothes, and like the old days, I stood in front of my room
mirror and tried to search for an idea. There was no news from
him or his spontaneous ideas. That time, maybe, I needed him
more than any other time, but as I had sent him to exile to the
deepest darkness of my inner self, I was sure there would be

no news from him any longer! I felt stupid. I couldn't focus for a minute. It was me: the helpless Amir—lacking any idea and alone!

After hours of thinking, the only thing that jumped in my mind was to say that I was selected and that the tall man wanted me to test for a great project. That way, maybe, my friends would believe I had unique traits and take me more seriously.

The next day, as soon as I entered the school, they gathered around me, and started to ask me questions seriously, as if they had money owed to me. After a little quibbling, I said: "It's not your business, it's mine. I have been selected." I really had stress. I didn't believe I could stand it for more than five minutes. I thought it was possible that I would gaffe any moment, and all my friends would realize about my false story.

"What do you mean that you had been selected?" Cody asked.

I must confess that I had no answer at all. After a long pause, I combined my words and said, "Well, I've been different at school. A few persons, I don't know who, took some students under their surveillance inside and outside the school, to find out who was more different than others, and had the potential to be a member of the strike force".

Henry asked with a grim face and complaining tone: "Huh! The strike force! Are you kidding? You even can't pass physical fitness test. Which strike force? Related to which state organ? You mean, you're an army-man now?"

Before I even could think about an answer, Jacob made everything more complicated with a more difficult question: "Can you tell me exactly what difference or prominence you had that others didn't have? Why didn't they select me? What were their standards that they preferred you to me?"

Of course, he didn't talk so impertinently. Jacob was an African-American who not only was physically much better than me, but better than the whole class. I don't know if his athletic and muscular body was because of his trainings or genetics. He always believed that the reason he could not be so successful was his skin color, and discriminations against him. Even a few times, he was about to quarrel with the teachers.

I wonder if it was really so, or Jacob had become too sensitive, but I know that Mr. Smith the superintendent of the school was always looking for an excuse to punish Jacob. Even it happened that in similar situations, he had pardoned other students and only punished Jacob. Several times he threatened Jacob to suspend him from school. All over, Smith was a hateful person.

Nevertheless, Jacob truly deserved to be a member of any group where physical fitness was concerned. Anyway, I was a loser and just wished that those investigations would be finished soon. I had become jittery and unwittingly said: "You may ask himself." As soon as I said that, I caught my mistake, but it was late and I could do nothing about it. I had thrown myself off a valley with my own hands! They certainly got satisfied after hearing it, as if all their problems were solved.

I tried to retract my words, but it was no use. They didn't stop picking on me. At that moment, I had to tell them that the whole story was fake, but I didn't dare confess. The bad thing about lying is that once you lie, you have to lie again in order to cover the previous one. These lies continue in a series so that the ending of the last lie connects to the first lie, and the lies will be disclosed. Always, in telling lies, one should allow no follow-up to be possible.

At last, we decided that I talked to the tall man in advance and tried to get his permission to meet them. There were two basic problems. First, I have been spending much time with my friends recently, and because I had left them when I was busy exploring myself with him, it was considered a favor for them to have accepted me at their gatherings, so they didn't expect me to ignore their request.

Second, I really didn't have the power to set my viewpoints apart from theirs. Whatever existed in me was good but not extraordinary, and it convinced my friends that there was not a serious relationship between the tall man and me. I had a feeling that they were chasing me on my way back from school so that they could meet the tall man without any middleman.

Finally, after a day or two of keeping them waiting, I told them what I was expected to say! I told them that it had been agreed that they could meet the tall man and listen directly from him why they had not been selected for membership in the group, but depending on a condition that the meeting would remain hidden, and they shouldn't talk about it with anyone. They easily accepted.

I was really astonished when I used to ask them to do unusual things before. Now that their curiosity was piqued, they were ready to do everything. Of course, that situation made me a little upset. Maybe if they had paid the least attention to my strange requests, I wouldn't have to lie and do those things.

My last effort to brush them off was to give them a remote address so that they possibly couldn't find it, or they didn't have the permission to leave the city. It was not so! As soon as I said that the location is outside the city, the only thing they asked about was the exact address and the time to meet. I had no other way, and in the meantime, that damned fear had worsened everything. I just had to tell them once that I had all lied about it. However, nothing would change, and they would realize the truth.

After I saw no disagreement, I told them to stay at school on Friday after the last class so I could give them the address. It was Tuesday, and I had two more days to find an address! After school, I rode to the city skirts on my bicycle, took the west side, and continued on Martin Spring Drive. I didn't change my direction. Route 66 was on my right side, and Martin Spring Drive led to Eisenhower street, where I continued my way. If I saw Route 66 on my right, I knew I was not lost. I continued riding my bike until I reached where Route 66 and Eisenhower Street separate from each other.

I was no longer able to find my way back home. After seeing the first dirt road on the left side of the street, I turned left. I was a little scared. I was alone, and it was the first time I went there. The worst thing was that it was a dirt road. I continued riding until the road ended. It took me about 35 minutes riding from home to the place. Maybe my friends would fear the dirt road and change their minds.

I returned the whole way. The next day, I spent my time arranging the scenario on how to answer questions. It was of no use. Neither a good idea jumped in my mind nor I could concentrate on a certain idea and process it.

It was Friday. After the bell rang for the last class, I put a note slip on my desk, on which I had written the address, and left the class sooner than other students. The note gave the address and the time of the meeting which was at sunset. The reason I didn't mention the exact time of the meeting was because I wanted an excuse to leave them.

It was afternoon, and I had gotten the jitters. My friends were the last people I had, and if they rejected me after realizing that I had lied to them, I would be alone. I went to the place of the address before they did. The sun was about to go down. The road was so empty I wondered why they had ever made it. There were no houses or stores. Nobody moved around the road, and the oddest thing was that it had a name.

The first time I went there, I didn't realize the name of the road, but the second time, on the wall of a house at the beginning of the road, someone had sprayed the name 'Pool Holler Cave Rd.' It was a cool idea. I don't know whether I liked it because the name was sprayed on the wall of the house or because of the interesting style of spraying. Whatever it was, it remained in my mind.

It was about dusk, and I was waiting for them. I just prayed that they wouldn't come. It was sunset and few minutes passed. I was in my thoughts that saw a car approaching the place. Oh, my God. There was no way to escape. Behind me, there were many trees, and I didn't dare go inside the woods. There was no side road, either. I could guess from the angle of light from the headlamps of the car that it was a truck. It was approaching slowly toward me and scared me more.

I feared something bad was going to happen, but worse came to me. Before, I would have lost my reputation with my friends. Someone driving a truck at the end of the road can't be an ordinary person. I changed my prayer and asked God to save my life.

The truck got so close that its headlights burned my eyes. I laid my hands above my eyes and the light to make a shadow for my eyes to see. The truck stopped in a few yard's distance from me. Three persons got out of the two doors, and three others from the cargo bed. I couldn't identify them, but the fact that they were so many was not good news.

I was gasping for breath and could see their shoes. Wait a minute! Their shoes looked familiar, but not all the shoes, of course. They stood in front of the car, blocking the headlights. I brought down my hand and could see them. Cody, Henry, and Jacob were the three persons I saw, and the other three were John, Josh, and Sam.

John was Cody's cousin, and Josh and Sam were his friends. They used to be together just like me, Cody, Henry and Jacob. They were seniors and were two grades above us. I had told my friends not to tell anybody else. So, what were they doing there? Ah, what a silly question. It was clear that they had told them.

Well, it was not so bad when I thought I would lose my life but worse than my first thought that they would realize my lie. In that case, I could at least keep it among ourselves, but in the new situation, more people would possibly be informed.

John, who was so devoted to Cody, looked around, came toward me, and slapped me so hard on my ear. Then he pushed me, and I fell on the ground. They gathered around me. At that moment, I was a loser. John said angrily, "Why would you make my cousin come to such a dark place to hear such stupid stories?"

I understood that they had gotten to know the whole story. I had no answer to give. John stared at me for a few seconds, then he took me by my collar and lifted me up. It's true that I'm a little slim, but he was really strong, too. "If I see you put someone's life in danger again and make them go to such places, I'll settle my account with you!" John said with a menacing tone.

In the meantime, Sam came forward and separated us. He was a slim black guy who, during the three years I knew him, always wore the same style glasses. John, who was pretty popular at school, received Sam's help in his lessons, and if someone caused any trouble for Sam, they had to face John. Josh was John's only novice.

"What are you doing, John? You don't let him talk." Sam said.

"Let him talk? You haven't believed the nonsenses of this stupid boy, have you?" John said to Sam.

"I didn't say I believed it. I am saying let him talk." Sam replied.

John turned to me and said, "Ok, Talk!"

I shook myself in order to buy time and think of what to say. "That man left here. They were supposed to come alone," I said in a calm and broken tone.

John frowned and said in a lifeless tone, "He left? Where to?"

I gulped my saliva and lifted up my head and shook it a little, when Sam quickly pointed while saying, "Just there! I told you John. The car at the beginning of the dirt road abruptly moved. Maybe, it was him."

I didn't mean anything by shaking my head but to gulp my saliva easily. By doing so, they thought I was pointing to the back of their heads. John, who had cooled down a little, cheered up and said with a firm voice, "OK. No problem. Prove it!"

Only a divine hand could help me. All were staring at me, waiting for a reasonable answer. For a moment, just for a moment, I closed my eyes, clenched my fists, and cried out loud from within. None of them heard the voice in my head, clearly.

I had already gotten tired. I needed help. I wished to return to the period when I had no fear of anything and made the best decisions in every situation. I needed a *he*! I cried out from within in such a way that *he* heard it from the depth of my soul's darkness and reached him from the remotest point of my soul to my mind. Then, *he* took control of my mind without asking for any permission.

Now, I was no longer alone. Yeah! My cursed one had returned! My tone changed from that terrified mode to a very calm and cold-blooded one. My mind began to process the moments I had already experienced and paid no attention to anything else. I didn't believe that my mind was so powerful. All of a sudden, I remembered that I saw a sign engraved on the trunk of a tree on my way to that place before sunset when still we could see things, so I quickly said, "A few yards back, there's a sign on a tree that shows our appointment was there."

"So, why didn't you make the appointment there?" John said.

I immediately answered, "Because it was part of the plan. We always used to set our meeting place to be after the sign so that we could avoid any danger. The group who knew the sign would stop and hide there, and when the other group passed them by, if they were members, would stop and wouldn't carry on to the place of appointment. Otherwise, if they passed by inattentively, it would be clear they weren't a member of the group. Anyway, our meeting place was there, but yours was here so it'd remain hidden."

I was amazed by such an offhand answer. Henry, Jacob, and Cody were looking at me as if they were watching a movie! They were all shocked. Josh scratched his head and said in a confused voice, "If all that was part of a plan so that we couldn't find it out, then why did you just talk about it?" It was a good question, and I really had no answer for it, but *he* did!

I abruptly said, "Because it doesn't matter anymore. He has left and won't come back again. It makes no difference for him since the plan is already disclosed."

Sam said disappointedly, "John! I told you that a 15-year-old boy can't patch up such a story, didn't I? We lost the chance to meet him."

John, who didn't want to give up, turned to Sam and said, "It's all lies. I didn't expect you to be fooled by his words."

"You told me to prove it. OK, let me prove it." I said.

"Yeah! Prove it. Get on the truck and show us," John said in an opportunistic tone.

I put my bike in the bed of the truck and sat with Cody, Henry, and Jacob. John, Josh, and Sam got on the car. We drove back, and I knocked at the rear windshield to stop when we got there.

We all got out of the truck, and I showed them the sign engraved on the tree. It was a circle with a multiplication sign in it. I truly didn't know what it could mean. Sam touched the sign like a detective and said, "It's almost old and can't be made today." I was lucky, as it made my story more believable.

John tried to change the atmosphere. He raised his voice and said in an angry tone, "It's all rubbish. It doesn't matter if these nonsenses are believable. I'll make you regret if I see you again with my cousin, trying to deceive him."

"Don't worry. I will talk to nobody," I said gently.

"It's OK because it must be so!" John said.

We got on the truck again and drove back from Phelps County to Rolla. On the way, nobody talked; we sat, just looking at each other. I didn't think it one percent probable that the whole story might turn that way. This time, I could have a word to say forever because of *him*!

Sam and John were arguing. Occasionally, Sam turned back and looked at me through the rear windshield. The cool thing was that he thought positively about my story. His passion to believe my story remained in my mind.

FIRST CIGARETTE

In the interrogation room ….

Jill, who was a little doubtful, said, "You said you saw a sign engraved on the tree like a circle with a multiplication sign inside it, right?" Amir nodded his head as a sign of confirmation. "Can you draw that sign for me on the paper?" Jill continued.

For a moment, Amir looked for the pen and paper that were on the desk, when Jill quickly pushed an opened notebook to his side. In a few seconds, Amir drew the sign and pushed it back to Jill. Jill was amazed to see the sign, intended to say something, but changed her mind in a moment. She stared at Amir for a few seconds and said, "Haven't you possibly heard the story of Zodiac?"

- "Yeah! I've heard something. Did you catch that insane man?"

- "The case is still open, but it's interesting that the sign you drew is very similar to the Zodiac sign!"

"The sign inside the circle I drew is like the letter 'x', but as far

76

as I've heard, the Zodiac sign has a plus inside the circle. Also, the crossed lines of the plus sign pass the circle, but the multiplication sign I saw didn't get into the circle." Amir explained.

"Have you ever read the book *Zodiac* by Robert Graysmith?" Jill asked.

"No, why?" Amir said.

"The suspect in Zodiac was capable of writing with two hands. It's so odd that your handwriting was different from the personality hidden within you!" Jill said.

Amir smiled coldly and said: "Yeah! Zodiac used to write with both hands. That's why his handwriting was different, but I write two different handwritings with just one hand. This is a mind capability by which you can control nerves in your mind!"

"Wait a minute! You said you haven't read Robert Graysmith's book. How did you know that he used to write with both hands?" Jill asked.

"I don't remember where I read it. That book was not the only information source of the group, but that doesn't matter. What matters is that I have the answer to the unanswered questions of the Zodiac case!" Amir said.

"And what's that?" Jill asked.

"Ghosts!" Amir replied after clearing his throat.

Jill, who seemed to be somehow confused, said, "What? Ghost? How is ghost related?"

Amir interrupted her, "The problem of the police was that they were chasing the murderer. They had to look for the ghost behind the case. The whole time, you were looking for a person hidden behind Zodiac's character, and this was exactly your mistake. To me, Zodiac is a goal. It's the name of a group, not a person. Those ciphers were made by a person. Maybe, the one who identified the murdered people had been a different person, and the one who killed was some other person, too! That's why the clues never matched! The handwriting, fingerprints, and mysterious character couldn't be collected in a single person. That's why I say that it was not one person and that each part was done by another individual. Don't forget that a person could be killed, but the ghost is not a goal to be perished!"

Jill, who didn't even believe to hear such words uttered from Amir's mouth, said in articulate words, "Don't you think all this information and conclusion is a little bit more than expected from a 25-year-old young man?"

Amir couldn't stop laughing and began cackling in such a way that Jill felt a little uncomfortable. He hardly stopped laughing after a few seconds and said, "Sorry. It was so good. These words are too much for me? I formed the group 'Smokers' when I was about 15 years old. You deem a simple conclusion to be out of mind? You have to listen to the whole story in order to understand the man I am, not as newspapers wrote it."

"Excellent! I am excited to know you through your own words. I'm here for this, of course. Well, what happened after you returned home from that place?" Jill asked.

In the story …

Before anything, I had to decide what I was to do—I had to decide what I was to do with *him*! In the summer, as much as I did my best to be like him, it was no use. After I sent him back to the depth within myself, there was no trace of those weird behaviors anymore.

I understood that I was persuading myself that we were mingling together. In fact, I were always myself, but because *he* had gotten more free, I didn't sense the difference between my will and his. However, *he* had saved me from the worst dilemma of my life.

Wait! Maybe all that happened was his own will, and *he* was just pushing me against that path so I had to call him for help again, and *he* could gain control of my mind. Maybe and maybe not! Anyway, it didn't make any difference because *he* had enough strength to guide me indirectly, and I didn't have the right to choose. Good or bad, I had accepted that he was an inseparable part of my life.

That night, as always, I stood in front of my room mirror and stared at myself. Different thoughts occurred to me, and I wondered which one belonged to me and which one belonged to him. On the one hand, I had really missed him before, and on the other, I hated my loser personality. I was not in a situation to deny his presence.

I decided not to quarrel with him and tried to be friends. In ordinary times, I had to take control, and in the time of adventure or when everything was unfavorable and tough, *he* had to steer my body's vessel! I sensed no opposition from within, either. Gradually, my life turned the way my body was in my own control when I did my daily routines, and *he* later took control of my mind.

It's not a pleasant feeling when your body is rented to two different people a day. However, it was not so bad. I always wished to be special. Now I had become so special that there was no similar instance like myself. Let me tell you something: If you are falling, try to somersault a few times before striking the ground and getting splashed. This way, you will benefit the most from the situation.

Of course, it wasn't such that when I was busy doing

something, I would ignore his presence. I didn't do something that would require him to correct all my works. For example, as I said before, '*he*' was very sensitive. I didn't do my homework in such a way that when *he* came to my mind at night, *he* had to write it again with good handwriting. I always made my room tidy, too. I repeat, again, it was not that I didn't have any control when *he* appeared at night.

I was responsible for all my words and deeds because my body moved under my command. It was more as if I had two vigilances, and occasionally, one of them gave me a new vision.

Anyhow, at school, John was always watching me at to see if I would go to his cousin to deceive him, but I was totally changed. I talked less, but when I talked, they were usual words. They didn't let themselves talk about that night, either. Of course, a few times, they intended to put forth the case, but I severely opposed to it and finished the argument before it started!

I wondered if they had believed my words, but I know they didn't look at me the same as before and even took the way of my walking under care. This was what I already wished for, but it was as if my priorities had changed after his return. Now I wasn't only satisfied being the group leader of a few friends. While others had taken me under their care, I, too, had Sam under me. My account was so believable to him as if he wanted to believe its truth.

But why? What part or piece of my vague and meaningless story had made him so enthusiastic? I had the same thoughts that he unwittingly gave me the clue. One day, I was looking at him in the school yard when one of his classmates jostled him while passing him by. Sam paid no attention and walked a few steps back to avoid any contact with him, but his classmate began arguing.

His classmate said that Sam didn't have to bump against him

because he is a black stinker. Sam had lost his temper and punched him in the face. All the students gathered around them. I don't know where John was. Mr. Smith, the superintendent, appeared there. As soon as he saw the guy bleeding from his nose, he grabbed Sam's shirt and said that school is not a place for tribal living, and no one has the right to beat another.

I don't know what he meant by "tribal living," but once Sam intended to defend himself, Mr. Smith shouted at him and told him in a disgusting tone not to talk anymore and to go to his office. Sam, who was broken down, talked to himself while going to Mr. Smith's office: "How come there's no one to listen to me. Where is the justice? I can't tolerate this injustice any longer. Is there anybody to listen to us?"

At that moment, I looked and was dumbstruck by his words. I didn't know why, but I knew that those words were not because of rage or nervousness. I believe that people tend to show their real self in anger. All their masks, pretentions, and behavioral lies are washed away when they become angry and reveal the purest part of their being without any prudery or pretention.

However, whether Sam's words were because of anger or thought, they were very heavy and painful. There were very few students who liked Mr. Smith. I'm not sure if his colleagues at school were friends with him or unwillingly tolerated him.

After school finished, I went back home. I lied on my bed, and as a habit—I don't know if it was my habit or *his*—I began to review my daily routines. Once I remembered Sam, I froze and recalled his words and his helpless face.

I was thinking about him, considering the unusual thoughts jumping in my mind. Three images appeared in front of my eyes. First, it was Sam's face. Second, the appearance of that tall man. Third, the image of the Lady Justice, Iustitia, a blindfolded woman with a sword in her left hand and a scale in her right hand.

But what relationship was involved in between all these? Well, of course, it's simple. Lady Justice is clearly a symbol of Justice, and Sam was talking about it What about that tall man? Oh, no! I really missed his ideas. Well, Sam made us all astonished. He was frantically trying to confirm my words and was complaining about injustice, too!

He was possibly looking for a person capable of making changes in the city. But I knew, if no one knew, that the whole story was fake. I had not talked to the tall man even once. I didn't know what he was doing, either. Wait! The point may exactly be here. The tall man I'd made had no external reality at all! Maybe, I could play his role—but how?

It's impossible. Even if I wanted to continue the play, I would be exposed, and others would realize that there was no real character behind it. I read somewhere, "The bigger the lie, the more people believe it." It was his highest power and skill to achieve a valuable relationship out of all *he* had seen and heard even if irrelevant and apparently unimportant.

Experiences of my life that were merely composed of dusty memories were turning into greater ideas, and *he* was a skillful master. The most valuable lesson *he* taught me was that anything apparently worthless may become efficient in a certain time and situation. Maybe, I could never imagine that this latter thought would be the reason behind strange and great works in my life.

I took an unused notebook to use only for writing such ideas. It was a red notebook with golden lines on its cover. The cover was thick and inflexible, and there was no title or name like 'notebook' on it. It was like a book with blank pages. I don't exactly remember where I bought it or whether it was a gift from someone; anyway, I liked it and had decided to use it in my best and most important class and to keep it for later times.

 I used to write down the ideas on my draft notebook, and after editing them, I transferred my revised texts to the red notebook. Before I intended to go into details, I had to finish my story.

I didn't know exactly what to do and whose role to play. Did I have to make myself seen or not? I think it took about two weeks of around-the-clock for me to create ideas in order to compose a perfect story. Frankly, the distance between *he* and I was gradually decreasing. I had known him already and didn't fear him any longer. I gradually got to understand him and agreed with what *he* did.

We reviewed our memories together and noted down some useful points. I was not sure yet if it was possible, but I was busy doing something, and I was not in a mode of routine. I remembered that I once had a close shave. A joke may be funny once and worth hearing, but the second time, it becomes lame. Likewise, my scenario could possibly finish unpleasantly and lame.

But I had a sense that if one told a joke in such an emphatic, firm, and frenzied way, people would laugh at it out of lunacy. So, I had to tell this joke so seriously and orderly that the people would be addicted to it. In the first step, you shouldn't think on how others react; you just have to do it seriously.

I knew I couldn't make it out alone, as I passed my whole summer on exercising my skills and couldn't be the best in any of the fields. So, I had to choose the best guys or people were better than me. In the meantime, I had to choose a name for the group. Since the tall man, wittingly or unwittingly, was the reason behind the forming of the scenario, I tended to think about him and his special style so that I would get inspiration.

I remembered the moment he was smoking in the park, and the good feeling I had while looking at him came back to me. That's why I chose the name 'Smokers' for the group, though I didn't have an interest in smoking. I also chose the title 'Justice and demanding right' as the goal of the group. The title popped up unconsciously.

When the image of Sam appeared before my eyes, I had a sense that someone should have done something for him. So, the tall man was there to do something! All people are looking for a savior, neglecting that they are saviors of their own lives. Well, there's no complaint! They were looking for a radiant man, and they got him.

Yet, I didn't know anyone to recruit as a member. It was too late for a slavish obedience. There was no tall man, as I had created in my story. My story could be valid if there was an indirect relationship among members. Before, when I used to socialize with my friends, I had tried to set up a group and gain its leadership.

Now that I had gained self-confidence, there was a difference. Before, I couldn't make it because of my fresh teenage members, but now grown-ups would cause it to triumph. This time, I would narrate my story only to those who were waiting to listen, not everybody! If you want to get a favorable result, you must proceed through those who belong to it! I got to know this because of my careless friends!

Sam had the potential to believe my story, but I needed more than one or two members. The bicycle repair shop where I used to work was located at Faulkner Avenue and next to a coffee-shop near the cross-section of Ridgeview Road and Bishop Avenue, the basic routes of Rolla. At the opposite side of our shop, there was AutoZone store with almost 10 years of good business. Nearly everyone who needed a car repair, went there.

Well, it caused me to get familiar with more people there. I usually repaired bicycles in front of the door of the service shop, so I had a good view for watching people and knowing them better. Before, I used to go the wrong way so that others got to know me, but this time, I understood that I had to know them so that I would introduce myself in an acceptable way.

From then on, my feelings about life and the world gradually lost their color, and I had the sense that the key to success lied in having no dependence on anything. If something is important to you, the stress of not achieving it will prevent you from having full concentration in life. This time, I was looking for nothing beyond my goal. All my pride and reputation would reach to a person who didn't have any external reality, though I had created my imaginary character, which was inspired by a real one I had seen. I couldn't show off, as it would ruin my whole story. Maybe it didn't matter anymore. Why did I do it when I couldn't reach my most important goal, the fame?

My days passed as before but meaningfully this time. I tried to watch people accurately every day I went home or to work. In the meantime, I used to write any useful words or quotations that I heard in a TV program or read in a magazine. I also watched a bank robbery movie to find out how the members divided tasks between among themselves.

Though I had a positive motive for this group, but I acted in a hidden and mysterious way in order to conceal part of the truth. As I couldn't make a direct contact with anybody, fearing they would realize that a 15-year-old boy is a member, I couldn't exactly say who was eligible for membership of the group. So, until I could recruit needed members, I made use of all that I gained. Needless to say, I knew the people to recruit and what conditions they should have.

My biggest problem was I didn't know whether I had to complete the book or prepare the rules for the upcoming events. So, I slowly moved forward to see which one would first show me the way.

Finally, after a few weeks of thinking, I made my decision to begin with Sam. I knew where he was living but didn't have his exact address. The next day, I followed him home from school and got his address, but it was not enough. I couldn't send him an invitation letter to his house. I had to find his room's window and make sure no one else was inside. It was not so difficult. I just had to wait behind his room window and hope he wouldn't draw the curtain.

One night after finishing my work at the service shop, I went to his house and found him doing his homework in his room. I had to deliver my message to him without being seen. We didn't talk with each other at school. In fact, I didn't talk to anybody, and even Cody, Jacob, and Henry distanced themselves from me. I wonder if it was because of John or if it was because they themselves were not willing to talk to me. Of course, it didn't matter when they were of no use to me anymore. Sam was my goal, and I just had one step to get to him. I deeply prayed to God that he wouldn't be so foolish to be scared and shy away. Anyway, I went back home and wrote this letter:

> "Hi Sam! This is the man you followed, Amir, to see him. My absence there didn't mean I was unaware of the whole account and what happened that evening. I'm called 'the tall man.' I was born in total darkness, and all my effort is nothing but to destroy my birthplace. The bitter taste of injustice has always been the flavoring of every moment of my life. I know what a bitter experience it is when a cruelty turns into a habit! I am everywhere while I'm nowhere! I don't know what Amir has told you, but no one has a direct relationship with me. He couldn't keep the secret, though he had the potential to do it. Never talk to anybody about my connection with you or you 'll lose

your chance to be a member. Particularly, try to behave naturally before him, and if he comes to you, don't ever talk about this. He is no more a member. Of course, be careful! Maybe I've told him the same things about you, and this might be a test. Maybe you both are under surveillance by a third member! If you ever decide to find me, you'll just waste your time, because you'll never do it, and seeing me is not worth it. What matters is the goal and the reason of my presence here in your lovely city, Rolla! The 'Sun of Justice' will again rise from the farthest point of the world, and this time, it will be forever! But, we have to begin from small cities so that the people will taste the pleasant flavor of justice and remember what a valuable thing they have lost. Destroying this capitalistic system that—like a huge monster—is devouring the whole human resources. The greatest revolutions have started by farmers and from the smallest villages. Don't you want to be one of those farmers and help bring back justice to your people? Isn't it worth being sacrificed for the cause of human values when sooner or later, the whole world is overwhelmed by darkness and immoralities? We are watching you, and first, we will bring justice back to you. Then you'll decide if you want to be a member of my group, the 'Smokers.'

I didn't know whether to put the letter inside the envelope or not; suddenly, the tall man appeared before my eyes. Of course, thanks to Hossein, who used to help me with his brilliant ideas on time! When I began to write the letter, *he* reminded me not to write it in my own handwriting so that it couldn't be recognized. All over, I decided then to write all letters in his handwriting.

Anyway, I rolled the paper like a cigarette paper, then pressed it with my thumb so that it was tightly folded. As it was my first step, I was a little stressed, but I didn't hesitate to do it. I set the alarm on my watch for 3:00 in the morning. After I got up and got dressed, got on the bicycle I had taken from my boss in the service shop. I rarely used that bike, but I knew that I would use it more in the future because timing was very important, and I didn't have a car to cover long distances in a short time.

Rolla was not a big city but going out at midnight for a boy my age was not safe. I reached his house, knocked at his room window a few times, put the letter behind the window, and began to pedal the bike until I turned to the next alley. I was very careful not to pass a pothole filled with water or mud so that my bike's tire track wouldn't remain on the ground. I hid behind a house and kept my eyes on his window. Occasionally, I looked around so that no one would see me.

He seemed to be in a deep sleep. I was gradually getting disappointed and took a few steps toward his window. Something was shaking behind the curtain. I quickly returned to the back of the wall and hid myself. Sam opened up the window and took his head out of the window and looked around with his drowsy and languishing eyes. He found no one, turned back his head, and was about to close the window. With his half-sleep eyes, he seemed unsure if what he was saw was real or a dream. Luckily, he took the paper and closed the window. Fearing that someone might have seen me, I returned home and went to my room.

Just as I closed the door of my room, my father got out of his bedroom. I was lucky he didn't see me. I had to wake up at midnight that year to proceed with my plan. My father used to do his prayers early in the morning. This is what the people of my country used to do. I lied on my bed but couldn't sleep till morning. I was thinking about the possible things to happen. It was either of the two: Sam would play my scenario, or he wouldn't believe it and would disclose my plan at school. In that case, I would be in real trouble at school until the end of the school year. There was no middle ground.

The next morning, I tried to behave naturally at school. I was looking for him at the school yard when we suddenly saw each other from a long distance. We both stared at each other as if we were frozen. I couldn't guess what he meant by that look. Was he thinking that how foolish I was to think that he would believe my story? After a few seconds, he turned his face very normally and joined his friends.

I was not sure whether he had believed me or not. Maybe he wanted me to continue the play so that in a proper time, he would catch me in the act. A few days passed, and he totally ignored me. I was feeling a little bold one day, so I intentionally bumped against him and pretended as if it was unintentional. I apologized and tried to initiate talking. First, I asked about the school and homework, and he gave short answers in a normal manner. Then I said, "By the way, Sam, I wanted to tell you something about that night..."

I had not finished my words when he turned to me and said in an impatient tone, "What are you talking about? It is all gone. Forget it. I don't want you to explain anything. Just leave it at that. I'm not willing to hear it. It doesn't matter if it's true or a lie." By these words, he showed that he didn't want to talk about it and had totally believed the story. Well, my mind was at ease with him, but there was no time to rejoice because from there on, I had to start recruiting more members.

Making the people preferably older than my schoolmates was a smart move. By the way, as age increased, the idea of 'Smokers' for the guys in my age turned to be more unbelievable. The elders may do bigger things, but they are less flexible than younger ones.

BOOK OF LAW

The biggest point was my book. I had to complete it in order to find the final framework. After my mind was at ease with Sam, I began to think about the ways to complete my book. As very few people had a cellphone at that time, the book could be the means to link them, provided that all had access to the same book, and the book had to be hidden in a way that only members were informed about the place.

Then I thought about how book could be a means of connection. Because if it happened that someone lied in wait for me, and I went to pick the book he would identify me. Thus, a second person who knew me had to take care of the book while not permitting anyone to be present when I went to it.

The work was getting harder because if anyone identified me, everything would be ruined, and there was no need for anyone to identify me. I told myself, "Well, we will think about it later! Before anything, we have to make the contents of the book clear; after that, we will think about the bookshelves!" I've really no idea if I was talking to myself or *him*! Frankly, my lifestyle was so mingled and combined that making any difference between things was impossible.

I could say I had taken the middle course, and *he* didn't do anything to make me embarrassed when *he* showed up at nights. We both had nearly become one. When an idea popped up in my mind, I wrote it down on a piece of paper and worked on it to see if it was conformed with the previous ideas. If it was so, I just added it up; if not, I compared it to see if my new idea was strong enough so that I could ignore the previous ones and reorganize the structure of the group. Vice versa, if my new idea was not good enough, I would remove it and look for a better way. In early days, I took the ideas forward.

According to that, I assigned a responsibility to myself and pretended to be a member invited by the tall man, so that no difference would be felt between me and the other members. Later, it occurred to my mind that there should be someone to observe the group from outside. Even if a member was assigned the responsibility to make a report of their mission, it would be possible for them to forget or ignore something about themselves. Who would be better than me? In the case of someone seeing me around the place of the mission, they would not suspect that it is me.

This way, I could approach the group during the mission as much as I wished, and no one would suspect a teenager. As it was a useful idea and tickled my fancy, I decided to rearrange the structure of the group. I even canceled my membership so that the members couldn't identify me.

I got inspired from everything around me, and in a way, I tried to make use of it in my group. I understood that if I wanted to accept adults as members, I had to design the scenario so no one would doubt me.

I watched more movies and read more newspapers. I even

used a point from the Pacman game when I played at the arcade. In the Pacman game, when Pacman exited from the left side of the screen, he immediately entered from the right side as if the two sides of the image were interconnected. The idea I got from the game was that 'Smokers' had to act like Pacman. The group had to draw the attention of the police, people, or anyone except the members.

The second phase of the mission began in a place devoid of any danger or attention, where the members would enter and carry out the mission with less danger. One day when the Robin Hood cartoon was being aired on TV, my attention was drawn by Robin's actions.

Robin Hood didn't work alone to earn money in order to help the poor but stole money from the wealthy people and distributed it. So, merely helping was not enough. He took the money from the plunderers and passed it to the poor so that justice would return to the city. That way, money and wealth would be well-balanced.

This non-centralized power could be a hidden goal of Robin Hood. I used that idea to set goals for the group. However, the most important point to help me form the group was the 'Conservation Theory' that I had learned in physics class.

In the interrogation room:

Amir, with his fingers interlocked, turned to Jill and asked, "Do you know what made a young boy capable of bringing people under his control and make them do what they wouldn't do on their own?"

"Surprise me! I think that's your favorite thing to do" Jill said.

Amir smiled and said, "My pleasure." He then moved his chair a little and sketched on the table with his finger while saying, "I always thought that a person should have gained so much power to be able to rule or to command others. As I had gotten the habit of building the bases of the group and making rules out of everything, I happened to realize that there is a relationship involved.

For example, suppose that a certain amount of power is required to lift a piece of stone. An individual may not be able to produce the required energy to do it, but the same piece of stone could be easily and effortlessly lifted by a few people. The same amount of energy is applied in two different situations, and those few people do not apply extra energies, but because the energy is shared between them, they may accomplish the job.

I benefited from this law in physics to exert power, and I thought to myself that if I had to do something that the powerful people do, like controlling others, I would need a huge amount of energy and power, but it seemed impossible. Instead of exerting the power by myself, I would share it between several people, I would be capable of doing what a powerful king can do. The important thing was lifting the stone. It didn't matter who did it.

The energy and power needed to do great things is always constant. When it is impossible for one and is too heavy, it would be possible with the help of a few people. So, I decided to divide the power of the king between the members of the group so that we all lift the stone together! For the same reason, I avoided centralizing power in the group and let each member to decide on their own.

The biggest difference between a man and a robot is that the distance between a robot that works and one that doesn't work is within the codes of each and varies greatly. I didn't need to encode the people to persuade them do what I wanted them to do, but I just needed to act in such a way that they would believe they had to do it. I offered ideas to them, and they accepted. There was no compulsion, except that the style of my inviting them was tempting."

"Tell me exactly how you tempted them to follow the person they didn't see or hear while none of them were simple-minded members?" Jill asked.

Amir lifted his head, looked at the ceiling, got a deep breath and said, "Well, the point is this: Before I wanted them to understand me, I tried to understand them. I believe that most people can solve their own problems, but they lack enough self-confidence. If their loved ones, or those they depend on, face a problem much bigger than their own problem, an unproven sense of devotion will boil up within them, and they will try to solve it.

I didn't solve problems. First, I carefully observed them to get a good understanding, and the small area of Rolla made it easier for me. I could solve their problems, then get to know their weak points. Frankly, I didn't solve any of their issues, but they managed to solve each other's problems.

The interesting thing was that they solved the problems of others even though their problems were more complicated. Meanwhile, I allocated the scores to myself so that they would get a feeling of dependency and increase their devotion. They, just like me, looked for someone to listen to them, someone who acted in a way that they would feel they are being paid due attention.

Well, I was the one who paid attention to them and gave them a sense of being important. They, too, voluntarily devoted themselves for the cause of the group. They suffered from a complex of attention, but the difference was I had the courage to accept it and managed to remove it, but they just denied it. The important thing is that in action, the truth turned to be something else. I proceeded in a way that anyone likes to be dealt with. I talked about poverty with the poor and justice with the oppressed. I understood the people well. That was the secret of my success."

"After all those years, if you find a second chance to be outside here and understand people, you will try to control them again?" Jill said.

Amir looked very secretively at the two security guards present in the room and standing behind Jill and said, "Why not? As I said before, I never tell a joke only one time for the people to laugh, but I repeat it until they weep because of insanity and excessive laughter, not because of its humor! Late today, you will get to know that nothing has changed since then except the fashion! To me, there's no difference between the first woman, Eve, and the present-day woman other than their hair style, clothing, and tastes. The origin of human nature has never changed. So, the answer for your question would be 'yes.' You just have to apply the needed formula, and that's it. But, before I want to say how I started to recruit members, I want to talk about the contents of the book *Smokers*."

In the story ....

My notebook had 100 pages, and I divided it into five different chapters. The first part, only two pages, started from the very beginning of the notebook and contained the reason and the goal behind the formation of 'Smokers.' The next part that started after the first part explained how to use the notebook. In part three, where pages were marked with English letters inserted at the bottom left corner of each page, the role of every member was indicated. The reason was because I didn't want the members to identify each other's names in the future.

I specified each member with a letter in an alphabetical order. When a member opened the notebook to find out their duty, they didn't need to browse the whole pages of the notebook, and they just searched the page where their membership letter was inserted. That made it easier for them to proceed further.

For example, when the first person in the group opened the first page of part three that started with the letter 'S'—the beginning letter of 'Smokers'—he had opened the fifth page of the notebook. As I tried to write similar to *his* handwriting, I applied too much pressure on the paper and left outlines on the page behind it, which made it difficult to read when one tried to write on the pages with raised surfaces.

For this reason, I wrote on the front pages and left the pages behind them blank. This way, reading became easier. In part three, where the responsibilities of every member were mentioned, I specified twenty pages anticipating that someday the number of members would reach twenty, though I was not so optimistic to even have three members in the group.

As my motto was that all members had similar shares in the, I offered 30 pages for suggestions, where any member could comment if they were dissatisfied with any injustice. After studying the complaint, I had to offer my final verdict.

The fifth and final part of the notebook was the work progress report, where every mission had a name specified with an English letter. For instance, the first mission was named 'Mission A' and included two halves. The first half offered a general explanation about procedures of the mission, and the second half included a progress report and a conclusion. Any casualties or other incidents about the mission had to be mentioned there.

I knew I had a difficult job to make the members believe my words. I had to think as great men do so that I could draw their attention. I spent time thinking about it and finally got a solution. Humans seek a relation and proof for everything. They would never believe something unless they observed it with their own eyes! But, in one case, they can easily discard an unanswered question without having any doubt about it or losing their belief in that thing.

It's almost a disturbing contradiction when you see those who find a pretext to reject something, but the so-called sacred things appear before it, and they leave all their doubts and accept it outright, though many unknown things have not been discovered yet! I used this trait of humans to consider the fifth part of the notebook for the sacred things so that adults would believe it more easily. In other words, the only time adults think like children is when sacred things enter the scene!

In the second part of the book it was noted that the book was somehow a 'record of deeds,' where accomplishments of the group and fulfilled missions were registered until the notebook came to the end and would be kept in a secure library archive. Later, when a world revolution happened, the book would be handed to the 'Savior' to consider the deeds of the members! I had no other religious reason to justify the case in part five.

It's to be noted that in the first half of the mission, only the sketches of the mission were explained, and details of the mission, like duties of the members, the time of the mission, etc., would be handed to the members in rolled pages so that they wouldn't have to refer to the notebook in case of forgetting things.

The rolled papers resembling a cigarette included information about each member. The blank page of the paper was rolled outside, and the written page was rolled inside so no one would identify the fake cigarette. It was a rule that members should have the fake cigarettes on their lips, and since they didn't light them, it was a sign for the members to identify each other, especially in crowded places.

I set aside the remaining pages of the notebook for the fifth part. Now, I had to complete the parts that didn't need members' presence. As the introduction for the first part I wrote the following:

Why 'Smokers'?

Hi! I'm the tall man. I've been called by this nickname so much that sometimes, I myself forget my real name! It doesn't matter what my name is. What matters is the deed behind a name that makes it a good name or a hateful one. Names, like everything else in the world, are nothing but a deceit and temptation! A worthless crust!

You are reading this text because you've been selected for a great goal. Hasn't the time come for you to draw the superficial curtain of this world and see its dark truth behind these false and deceiving beauties?!

Why do we live? Is the goal of life to do the same things our ancestors did? How meaningless is a life rotating in an orbit of repetition! Aren't you tired of all these daily routines? Now that this cruel world is filled with oppression and tyranny, it's the time for chaos! These people believe in good deeds, but the existing structure of the world has made them sleep. They need someone to awaken them.

Aren't you tired of sleeping? If you still feel thirst for justice and light within your soul, set off to join the 'Smokers'. Let the people see the dawn once more. If in case you are ready to cooperate willingly, not compulsory, turn the page, read the instructions of the group, and start your way towards light and the truth. Contrary to this oppressive world, we never exert any pressure on our members to join the group, and the membership is arbitrary, so there's no way to return in case you become a member. The question is: Who wants to fall asleep again after waking up and seeing the realities of the world?

I don't exactly remember how big I wrote the words of the introduction or whether I could insert the whole text in one page or had to continue onto the second page, but as I said, I left the even pages blank. Anyhow, I wrote the instructions on the next page as follows:

Welcome to 'Smokers'

Reading this page indicates that your awakened conscience has overcome your fear resulting from ignorance and that you are ready to have a share of future history. 'Smokers' is a group free of any dependence on any state or non-state organizations, and its goal is to prepare the underlying ground for the savior. This group may be called an anarchist group due to its goal based on deconstructing the existing sordid social system. As no victory is brought without proper plans and disciplines, there are certain rules or regulations within the nature of the group.

As a reference, there's an alphabet letter in the cigarette paper you already received; it indicates your name to the end of the mission. no one has got a name here because no one is important alone, and our goal is not fame! We strive to gain justice. Your duties have been mentioned in a page of the book according to the alphabet letter on your cigarette paper.

After reading your duties in the group, you must pick up the knife beside the book and cut your finger. You then have to leave fingerprint weltering in your blood at the bottom of the page. It is a sign that you will remain loyal to the goal of the group. A few pages forward, you will find the suggestions page. As a member of this justice-seeking group, you may write about any

oppression in the society that has turned to order.
We will duly consider it for further measurements.

Have in mind that our group is not a place for
settling personal scores with anybody, and it is
established set for a greater goal. It will be agreed
to consider the case if the oppression is
recognized as an obstacle to reaching world
justice. A week after your suggestion is placed,
our supervising agent will be informed about it. In
case of our agreement, the planner of the group
will manage to design a plan for the mission and
by drawing a burning cigarette informs that the
suggestion has been accepted and if on the
suggest page there is sign of no smoke, it means
it has been rejected. If that was accepted the plan
maker divides its duties between the members. At
the end of the book, you will find the most
important part of the book, the 'work progress
report'.

This is not an ordinary book. It will be archived as
a document verifying our endeavors for the rise of
the 'Sun of the Truth' and will be handed to the
savior.

On Monday, a working day, you must go to the
Rolla cemetery at the cross section of S. Rolla St.
and 72 Rd. On the north west of the cemetery, you
will find a blind beggar who sits there every
morning. He wears an old grey coat with its
pockets always open. On the back of his coat you
will find a small sticker. If the sticker holds your
alphabet letter, drop some money in the bowl in
front of him. While he reaches for the money, take
your rolled cigarette paper out from his left
pocket, then pluck the sticker off the back of his
coat and leave the place without being noticed.

The paper should not fall in one's hands, and no one should be informed about it, as it is a linking code between us. All the details of the mission have been written on the paper. Always keep in your mind that there shouldn't be any connection beyond the mission between you and other members. Even if another member goes to you and tries to get in touch with you without having informed anyone, it could be a test from our side.

Even if you have regular contact with them, approach them as a stranger. Remember that you will talk about the group with anybody only when you intend to completely ruin this hope of light and turn it to darkness. You will endanger your future in the group and destroy the lives of many defenseless children who might have a deserving future because of the group's fighting against oppression.

It's the beginning of the work. The 'Smokers' will gather from the farthest points. Never think about the next step, because you may have your own vision, but the group has a long-term goal. Don't let your daily life be affected by your night missions, and don't behave in a way that lets anyone detects a change in you and your life. When on a mission, put the rolled paper on your lips like a cigarette, but don't light it so you may be identified by other members.

Be careful when you see anyone with a cigarette on his or her lips if they are not smoking it. As mentioned in the first cigarette paper, the code of the group is the way two members ask and answer a question as follows: "Do you have a cigarette with you?" and the answer would be, "A cigarette to smoke or to read?" After the mission is

finished, burn your cigarette paper so no trace is left.

'Smokers'

Regarding cutting the finger and leaving a bloody fingerprint, I had a feeling that it may sound like a group with no danger, especially for a group that claimed to fight the oppression. This way, it would be more believable for everybody. The idea of the stickers and the beggar jumped in my mind because the Rolla cemetery was near my working place, and I had already seen the beggar several times.

A while ago, I heard two men talking about the beggar; one said to the other that the man had been begging for about six years exactly at the same place without being disturbed by anyone for begging. It didn't happen that he would be absent there even for one day. It made me think that who better than a blind man could be a liaison, someone who could hardly understand the happenings around him and would always be present at the same place.

Those days, not many people had cell phones, so there were much less contacts. There needed to be a go-between so that I wouldn't be identified by other members. I could also attach all the stickers on the back of the beggar's coat without him knowing. I had bought a lot of those little stickers with only alphabet letters on them from Walmart chain stores.

Rolla was a small city, and I had to think about the number of members of the group. In case of increase in the number, the possibility of the group to be exposed increased, too. The idea popped in my mind that I'd better recruit seven members, the equal to the number of letters of the name of the group 'Smokers!' Luckily, all letters of the word 'Smokers' are different, except the first and the last letter, the latter being a sign of a plural name.

So, I decided to take six members and think about what to do for the last letter. Thus, the first member was called 'S'. When he would see the sticker 'S' on the back of the beggar man's coat, he would reach for his left pocket and pick the rolled cigarette paper with the letter 'S' on it. The second member would pick letter 'M', the third one would pick 'O,' and so on. I had not yet decided about details of each member's mission; I mean, it was not yet clear for me what every member had to do while on a mission because I still had not recruited any members.

FIRST MISSION

I had another problem: I first had to exhibit myself so that it would become easier for the members to believe the group. It was not logical to invite all from the beginning and expect them to follow me without any dispute. I had to plan some trivial missions so that willingness for membership would be increased.

Later, I understood why I started that weird quarrel with my father. I could gradually understand Hossein. *He* was neither the child victim of the shark attack or the shark itself! He was the whole adventure, the whole story. It didn't matter to him if I was beaten by my father. What mattered to him was that everything would proceed the way he wished. Maybe, I was making a mistake from the beginning, and he was more looking for the ways to control things not just be famous.

Anyway, no score belonged to me. Maybe I caused some operations performed in my city, but I would never become known. My name was 'the tall man,' not my real name. I had no enthusiasm or fear. Every day, I got more insensible but more serious, too. I was often myself, and *he* just helped me when I needed his assistance and made my way forward with a pure idea and thought.

It didn't matter what would happen to me anymore, as any day could have been my last day. At my workplace, I looked at the people and tried to guess their capacity through their social behavior. For a few days, I used to do the same until I saw Mike talking with somebody at AutoZone car repairs. He was a young and athletic black man who was about twenty years old. He seemed to be a calm and quiet boy. We happened to talk to each other a few times at lunchtime.

One of his customers was busy talking with him. I was there for something and didn't want to disturb their conversation. I was close enough to hear what they said. Mike was very upset because of being moneyless and said that he needed 300 Dollars for getting his mother's medicine. He also said that he had begged to acquaintances and friends, but as Christmas was around, nearly all of them counted on their money for the new year expenses and couldn't be of any help.

Mike had to wait until the end of the month to get his salary and be able to buy the medicine. It jumped in my mind at a moment that I had saved about 500 Dollars. I decided to tell him that he could count on me, but *he* stopped me at once. I got to know the whole story. Mike had told his problem to quite a few people, and he couldn't track me through everyone—I was in a position to give him the money he needed and ask him to begin the first mission of the group.

Even I was not sure if he realized my presence. The ideas came to my mind in an odd way. To be more correct, it first occurred in *his* mind, and *he* transferred it to mine.

The next week, it was the Christmas party at school—nearly all the students were going to attend. I had already told Sam that 'Smokers' would help him because of the group's justice-seeking ideals and that he could join the group in case of his willingness. I was aware of his severe hatred towards Mr.

Smith. I would attend the party with Sam and Mr. Smith. Mike was ready to do anything for 300 Dollars. He would afflict a misfortune on Mr. Smith's second car, and as I would be present at the party, no one would suspect that it was me.

I went back home from work, took out 300 Dollars from the box that I used to keep my money inside, folded it, and put it in an envelope. I then wrote a text on a piece of paper, rolled it, and put the paper with the envelope inside a larger one and wrote: To Sam! The text on the paper read,

> Mike, we are living in a pitiful world, where a mother is in need of money for her medicine, while others are wasting money to buy worthless goods. Which one is more important: Good health of an individual or wearing colorful shoes?! What has caused such a gap? No one hurries up to help that mother. People are not guilty! They used to be good in the past, when they lived sound and simply. The frenzy of this decorative and consumerist world is the cause of distance between the hearts of people.
>
> You'll find 300 Dollars inside the envelope, which is enough for your mother's medicines. It's a gift, and you're not entitled to return it. If you want to be part of the people who wish for a healthier and safer life, please prove your good will. Are you sure that if you were not a black, the people would give you a negative answer, too?! In the following address, there lives a man who is considered one of the dangers of our city. He is guilty of discrimination and racism.
>
> Go to his house at 8:00 PM. You'll find a hammer and a spray bottle at the back of his yard. Spray the following text on his wall, "A black is the same as a white!" Then, spray the name of the

**group 'Smokers' above the text. You have one
minute's time: 15 seconds for spraying the text
and 45 seconds for smashing his car. If you
succeed in fulfilling the mission, we'll get in touch
with you again!**

'Smokers'

Early the next morning, half an hour before going to school, I
left home. On my way, I went to Mike's house, and I knew he
would be the first person to draw up the blinds of his window.
Thus, he would be the first person to see the envelope. I put
the envelope next to the door of his house and prayed no one
would be curious enough to pick it up. I went to school and
was thinking about how if Mike had gotten the envelope, he
would believe my message. Was it possible that he just took the
money and refused the mission?

I had no alternative but to give him the money first. This way,
I would give him confidence. It would become too late if I
wanted to give him the money after doing the mission because
he would take his salary before Christmas. After school, when
I went back to work, I realized that he had received the
envelope because he was so happy. However, nothing was
clear yet. I had to wait until Christmas.

In the meantime, I was also looking for other members to
recruit. Adam was one of those guys that really tickled my
fancy. He used to work in a coffee shop next to the service
shop where I worked. He was a slim tall boy with blue eyes and
short hair. He seemed polite, too. I had already been to the
coffee shop a few times.

He was 30 years old, and we didn't happen talk much with
each other. For this reason, I always tried to carefully listen to
him while talking to other customers so that I could know him
better. He seemed to be a little self-controlled and didn't talk
too much about himself. I don't know why I had a feeling that

107

he had the potential to be in my group, though there was no sign of willingness in him for doing weird things. I was so sure that I went there nearly every other day to have a coffee.

A few days passed, when one day, he suddenly asked me about my almost continuous presence in the coffee shop. I just mentioned the high quality of their coffee and my interest in coffee. He simply thanked me. I was worried if he was suspicious of me so that if I would invite him for membership he would think that I was behind all that account. At that moment, I began to think about going there less often or just dismissing his membership in the group. I was about to leave the coffee shop to go back to work that one of his friends, a student at UMR (University of Missouri, Rolla) entered.

First, I didn't pay much attention, but when I saw how warmly they intermingled, I changed my mind. They seemed to be sincere friends. I had never seen Adam so warm and friendly. I told myself that it was a good chance to get more information about him while he was talking with his sincere friend. So, I ordered my second coffee and totally forgot that I had to be at work in a few minutes.

They didn't call each other by name, so I couldn't get his name. They just talked about the university, and I understood that they were friends. Till that moment, I didn't know that Adam had studied at the university. His friend comforted Adam a little and tried to talk about good memories, but Adam continued with more bad news pertaining to the rent of the coffee shop; both he and his father couldn't afford the high expenses and had to close the coffee shop soon.

His friend, who was moved with compassion, sympathized with him. Adam was prepared to tell what he had in mind and almost chocked him with sorrow, "I respect destiny. Maybe some people are more talented than others or are in better conditions, but I feel disturbed to see that a teacher mediates for the scholarship of a girl who is likely cute, and who knows what kind of relationship exists between them outside the university? On the contrary, I always have been a diligent and hardworking student. As much as I entreated the authorities of the university to help and grant me a respite to pay my tuition fees, they paid no attention and rejected my request." Adam, choked with emotion and continued: "Even this coffee shop has the same story. Everything was going well until 'Hot Coffee' started its work in the city. We always have tried to do things right."

His friend quickly interrupted Adam and asked about any relation between his coffee shop's slacking and Hot Coffee's opening. Adam said in a louder and more violent voice, "Because they offer beer to high school guys and university students under legal age, and so many of them go there. They are more successful because they work illegally. This is a world of injustice. For example, look at this guy here. He is our customer."

Adam pointed to me with his finger and asked for my name as if he forgot my name. I was really confused and didn't think that he would feel my presence there, so I hurriedly answered, "Amir, buddy! My name is Amir."

He turned to his friend again and said, "Amir always comes here because of our excellent coffees, but the rest of the guys mostly go there. Most of our customers include young people."

I got happy that he didn't suspect me, as I already doubted. He totally saw me as a customer and could not even remember my name, and I was happy of my being there. I remembered that I had to return to my workplace; I paid for my coffee and got ready to leave. Adam, who had cooled down, thanked me more than before and said goodbye. It couldn't be better. In a few minutes, I'd got to know nearly most of his life background without any trouble.

I made a mistake, of course. It would be better than that

because when I got to the door of the coffee shop, his friend told him that if he missed his old friends, he could see all of them at a student party that was to be held in late February, when even David would attend. I knew David! He was one of the genius of UMR who had attempted to commit suicide a while ago, but his friends reached him in time and saved his life.

All over, the number of suicides at Rolla university was high, but as he was one of the elites with a different reason for suicide, it made more news than others. In the hospital after he woke up from anesthesia, he was asked if his suicide attempt was because of academic stress and pressure, and he had replied that he had done it because he had become indifferent.

Yeah! I said that it would be better. The reason was that David, too, would attend the party. Of course, at that moment, I didn't have any plan or idea about it. Adam was enough for me to get busy planning for the missions. Anyway, I remembered David had told in the end of his remarks that "It's a world of injustice!" As I had mentioned in our book, I first had to give him a hand from the group so that he would have a taste of justice.

I returned to work, and the entire time, I was thinking how I could be of any help to him. To get a better vision of the situation, I broke down the issue into smaller parts. I had no exact information to know if offering alcoholic drinks in coffee shops was against the law. Till then, I had not seen or heard that any coffee shop in Rolla sold alcoholic drinks. Of course, it didn't matter, because that coffee shop sold beer and alcoholic beverages to high school and university students under the legal age. I could just inform the police, but that didn't help.

Firstly, how could I give a score to 'Smokers' because of the help to Adam? For sure, everyone could offer that help. Secondly, the way Adam was disclosing his ideas, it was totally clear that because of any reason, he didn't want anyone else to be informed. That time, maybe because he had seen his friend and had got somewhat emotional, he had told something he didn't want to say. Plus, Adam could have called the police already. So, he had told it to no one else. This increased the risk of me getting exposed, and if he realized that anyone had informed the police, his friend and I were the first suspects jumping to his mind.

My last reason was that Adam's coffee shop was good but not great. In fact, I just told something to have the chance to go to his coffee shop again without being suspected, but he had taken my praises seriously, and so he seemed to be a pushover. Maybe the whole account about Hot Coffee was a lie, and he had just heard it from someone and believed it. In the meantime, it didn't seem that slacking of their job was because of some high school students.

Most of the customers of coffee shops are usually young adults. It's a coffee shop, not an ice cream shop! I remember some of my friends who drank even though they had not reached the legal age. For example, a friend of mine invited me to a place where he said that Susan would be one day—that place could be Hot Coffee! Anyway, I had to figure it out.

The next day, at school I didn't go to my friends because we didn't have a sincere relationship. Instead, I went to Susan. I didn't think it was possible that talking to Susan would cause me danger in the future. As I had seen her with another boy, I thought she was not interested in me and didn't think about me. I told her to wait for me after school because I wanted to have some words with her. She accepted with a smile.

After school, I saw her in front of the door, standing with a few of her friends. It was not good. I thought she would be alone. This way, I had to be careful about a few others. I went to her and noticed that she hadn't understood I was willing to talk only with her. It was my fault because I didn't tell her anything about that. Anyway, everything had changed. Now, even if we got alone, her friends would surely ask her what we talked about. I had no choice but to change the subject or look for another guy to ask if selling alcoholic drinks by Hot Coffee was true.

I could understand from her face how proud she was. She seemed to be willing to humiliate me in front of her friends so that she would be more darling in their eyes, but I was making a mistake. When I went to them, they all stopped talking and kept silent for me to talk. I said a brief hello. Susan said, "I think you wanted to tell me something, Amir. Of course, you could say it at school!"

"I exactly had a reason and a purpose not to talk about it at school, but you didn't get it!" I said sarcastically. Then, I pointed with my head to her friends. All over, I was not so popular among the girls at school, and what I already said deprived me of the little popularity I probably had! "I just wanted to congratulate you for your new relationship and wish you luck," I said and quickly left. As I was a few yards away, I saw Susan calling me and running towards me. I stood for her.

"Just that? You just wanted to congratulate my new relationship?!" She said.

I looked at her friends who still were standing there and looking at us and said, "Yeah! Just this, and of course wanted to tell you to be careful."

"What should I be careful of?" Susan asked.

"The place where you get drinks. It's a dangerous place." I answered, while outguessing so that if she confirmed, I would realize it was true.

Susan, who was a little confused, said, "If you mean the last school year when you saw me with him, I should say there's nothing between us. We just separated. In fact, there was no relationship. Regarding the drinks, you are making a mistake. I bring drinks from home; I don't accept drinks from anyone."

"You mean, you didn't buy beer from the coffee shop that guys usually get drinks?" I said.

"If you mean Hot Coffee, I've to say no! Not all the people know it. You don't drink alcohol at all. Then How did you know it? Even those who got beer from Hot Coffee kept it a secret so that it didn't go viral." She said.

"How in the world did you know it then?" I asked.

Susan raised her eyebrows and said, "Well, I heard it from my former boyfriend!"

"But you said that ..." I said.

Susan interrupted me at once, "I said I didn't drink. I didn't say that he didn't drink! Anyway, it's better we don't talk about it at all. I don't want old memories be repeated once more."

I apologized to her, said a simple thank you, and quickly went back home. I was so happy. I've no idea if it was because I got to know that Hot Coffee was selling alcoholic drinks or because I understood that Susan was in no relationship. A part of me was happy because of Susan being alone, while was delighted because I got the needed information without any trouble! And by now, you know which part of me was happy because of which news that I got.

The good point was that even when her friends asked her about my questions, she would talk about her relationship, not about my information on Hot Coffee. I had two reasons for this. First, she said that no one knew it, and we'd better not talk about it, so she didn't. Second, I raised the issue while talking about her relationship, so it wasn't probable that she paid attention to the rest.

I returned home and began planning the scenarios. If everything proceeded well and Mike fulfilled his mission, then I could ask Sam to do something for Adam. So, I had to postpone his mission until after Mike's had been completed. The question was now about how Sam could help me. I was not sure if he could do it alone. Maybe, I had to help him in a way he wouldn't realize. This way, he would believe that there were really some people behind the group.

The first idea that occurred to me was the funniest ever, but when I reviewed my all other ideas, I concluded that there was no other way but the very frantic one: setting Hot Coffee ablaze. The idea was a cinematic one, and the problem was that I was living a reality! Hossein, or better to say '*he,*' wanted to make life a movie, and that's why he welcomed all dangers and instigated me to be bold. I, too, was gradually getting used to it.

There were two weeks left until Christmas, and I spent one week arranging how to set Hot Coffee ablaze. The first two days, I was busy reviewing the map and visiting the area of the coffee shop so that I could have a complete and clear image for the operations. The point was that there were no other shops around the place, and the sidewalk was not crowded. Often, only customers of Hot Coffee used to cross the street.

Finally, after a thorough survey and watching the employees under surveillance, I got to know their routines. I was lucky to see a truck carrying a black package of bundle. One of the employees quickly picked up the bundle from the cargo bed and took it inside the shop; the truck left the place immediately. Susan was right. It was not the way school students make a queue to buy beer. If it was, someone would have realized the story in advance. Maybe that was why Adam did not call the police.

I set up the plan so that Sam had to draw the attention of the people and do something to make everyone leave the shop, then I would go inside and set the shop ablaze. This way, no one would get hurt. In the end, I would spray behind the wall and leave a trace of the group on it.

There were a few problems though. First, Sam would probably be suspected because as soon as the people went toward him, the shop would be set ablaze. I had to make some other guy busy so that no one would suspect Sam. I would also be in trouble because the coffee shop had just one door to enter and exit.

The first point, the most important one, was concerned with how I should set the shop ablaze. I couldn't enter with a gallon of gas in my hand without being noticed. I didn't have a car to hide the gallon inside the trunk. I was deep in thought, trying to find a solution when something of a divine hand popped in my mind. I was sure it was *he*!

There were for sure, alcoholic drinks inside the black bundle being kept in the shop, so all I needed was to find the bundle, break the bottles, soak the floor of the shop in drinks, and light a match—that was all! Of course, I shouldn't forget that I had to spray first, then go inside. Otherwise, all attention would be drawn to the shop, and I shouldn't be present that time. There remained many ifs and buts, but they were so much that I decided to ignore them and do what I planned.

Finally, Christmas arrived. On the second day of the holidays, I went to the school party as usual. Before going there, I left the spray bottle and the hammer that I had already prepared at the back yard of Mr. Smith's house. I tried to look normal, but I had to be seen by others, particularly Sam and Smith. So I made sure they saw me at least twice at the school party around them.

Everything looked good. After an hour I was gradually getting worried that something went wrong until when an agitated person entered the party and whispered something in Mr. Smith's ear. Smith's face turned red, and he left the place very quickly. The only thing I did was finish my soda with a smile and enjoy my moments of life!

OFFICIAL SMOKERS

The news leaked out sooner than I guessed. The next morning, four of my friends came to me to inform me about the happening the day before. It was weird because mostly I lost my friendship with others. Anyhow, in response, I showed them the 'city desk' page in a newspaper to let them know I was already informed about it. My dad got them since that was good practice for him to improve his English. They were astonished to find that a 15-year-old boy had read about the incident in a newspaper on the second day of the holidays break.

I think I got carried away too much and did something foolishly and cinematic. I decided not to have such hasty reactions afterwards. The newspapers had covered the story in the way I expected. Without thinking about anything, I set my watch alarm for midnight and went to Sam's home. As usual I put a cigarette like rolled paper behind his room window and after knocking at the window, I left the place. This time, I was so certain that even I didn't wait to see if he picked it up.

I couldn't wait for the feedback from the people in the city because I had to fulfill everything as long as people were in shock and couldn't decide what to do! The later I acted, the more cautious would people get. I had learned this from a book of magic tricks that said that the best time to perform a trick is when the spectator is distracted. So, if the people were distracted by Mr. Smith's car, I had to start the second phase of the mission.

I had explained details of the mission for Sam on the cigarette paper. Hot Coffee usually started their work four days after Christmas holidays, whereas two days had already passed. Sam had to go there with a plastic bag of water containing some fish he had already bought. When he reached the front of the shop on the opposite side of the street, he had to tear up the bag on purpose, and when the fish spilled on the ground, he would start crying out and asking for help.

People would probably go toward him to help, but it wouldn't last for more than a short time. I would go from the back yard—where I would spray on the wall—toward the door and enter the shop. I was hopeful to find the black bundle and break the bottles. This way, the whole floor would be covered with alcohol, and it just needed a spark to make a beautiful firework!

No one would suspect Sam because the fish were real, and everything would seem natural. I had noted on the cigarette paper that he should extend the process of the operation as much as he could. I didn't mention anything about my part. I just wrote that when the shop was set on fire, he wouldn't leave the place quickly to avoid being suspected.

I already knew that Sam had an aquarium at home, where he kept a lot of small fish. It was possible that his associates would suspect him after hearing the news. So, I put some money inside the envelope and asked him to buy some fish in advance, though I knew that most shops were closed during Christmas holidays. Sam owed this to Smokers after what I just did for him.

I went to the place half an hour before the set time so I could keep everything under control. Sam came in at the right time. I had two spray bottles. I left one at the back yard of Mr. Smith's house for Mike to spray on his wall. I took the second one with me. I had to keep it, not throw it away, so I would not get caught.

I went to the backyard of the shop and quietly watched Sam. He looked at his watch. It was 6:00 P.M. He started to walk at the other side of the street, opposite to the Hot Coffee shop. His face was clearly full of fear. I was lucky because it was a holiday and not crowded. It wasn't snowy, and my shoe prints wouldn't remain on the ground. I returned to the back yard of the shop and waited for Sam to cry out.

As soon as he began to shout for help, I started my job! I didn't have enough time to watch him again to see if everything went right. I sprayed a sign on the wall. It was like the traffic sign 'No Entry.' Next to the sign, I wrote, "Fire did not set the shop ablaze! Alcohol set it on fire. Sins set it on fire." To the right of the words, I drew a minus sign and the number 21. At the top of all, I wrote, 'Smokers.'

I was almost finished with spraying when I heard a dog walking around the place. I turned my face and saw it about 20 yards away from me. I also heard the footsteps of the dog owner getting closer to me. I shouldn't be seen. At the other side, I also heard the footsteps of Hot Coffee staff running towards Sam to help.

I quickly moved from the backyard to the door and entered the shop. I was a few steps inside the shop, when I suddenly heard one of the staff members loudly calling his colleague to bring a larger bowl because there were so many fish. It meant that one of them was returning to the shop and would probably see me. So, I quickly leaped under a table and dragged myself toward the side of it that was touching the wall, trying not to be seen.

He entered the shop in a few moments, and after searching behind the cash box, he found a large bowl. They were in front of the shop and would happen to see me if they turned their heads. I got out from under the table very quickly, went to the cash box, and started to look for the black bundle. It wasn't there. My whole body was filled with stress. Suddenly, as I was looking around, my right leg stumbled on a black curtain hanging on the wall and I felt something behind the curtain!

First, I thought the curtain was for decoration and that there was just the wall behind it. When I drew it aside, I noticed what was behind it! I found two black bundles there and quickly tore one with a knife that I found in the shop. Inside it were a few Barbie dolls. It seemed so odd for a coffee shop to keep dolls. What were the use of those dolls? I didn't have enough time to think on it, so I promptly opened the next bundle and found the bottles at last—what a relief!

I looked at the shop and saw them gathering the fish. I began to break the bottles by hitting them at the edge of the counter while pouring the drinks on the floor but quietly. I scattered the smashed glass around as a proof to my words. I suddenly heard one of them asking Sam if he needed any other help. I realized that they were finished with the job, so I took out the match, lit it up, threw it on the ground, and ran out of the shop. I went to the backyard to take my spray bottle and leave the place from the same side so that I couldn't be seen.

Immediately after I went there, I saw the dog standing with his owner—a boy about ten years old. We stared at each other for a few seconds. It could be the end of my story there since he had certainly identified me. I was discouraged. We kept staring at each other until he began making a gesture with his hand, and I realized that he was mute. I wondered what a mute boy with his dog was doing there on a holiday. It didn't matter to me, either.

My heart was beating so fast it felt like it was going to fly out of my chest. After a short while, when I felt less nervous, I quickly jumped over the wall of the park behind the shop and got away. As I was running, I heard people shouting, "Fire! Fire! Help! Fire!" I ran away more quickly and a few alleys away, I hid the spray bottle inside my jacket and started to walk.

I arrived home, went to my room, and lied down on the floor. I felt so dizzy that the chandelier right in front of my eyes seemed as if it was spinning round my head. I hoped that no one had seen me. Still feeling dizzy and watching everything in the room whirl around my eyes, my attention was attracted by a poster of Freddie Mercury, the singer of Queen.

Maybe it was an inaccessible wish for me to achieve his fame one day and shout like him in front of thousands of fans, but there was a point that could change the story! I dare say that at the moment I was lying on the floor, with all chemical reactions inside my body, I was experiencing the same pleasure that Freddie did on the stage.

Maybe, it didn't matter very much. The ultimate result of being famous and performing on stage is experiencing the pleasure that other people couldn't achieve because they possibly would never have the chance to be in his position. If you may enjoy on the ground, the same as he does on the stage, it doesn't matter whether you are on the stage or behind it.

While things were swirling around my head, I closed my eyes and enjoyed the excitement I needed throughout my life. I didn't hate myself anymore. I was no longer scared. There was no *he* anymore! Now it was me that dared to do things *he* wished to do! I was not aimless any longer. I didn't wish to be Freddie anymore, because I was the Freddie of my own life! I was Amir—the very Amir I wished for. No one could stop me anymore. I enjoyed my time and fell to the deepest and sweetest asleep of my life.

In the interrogation room …

"You mean, the group was formed that easily?" Jill said.

Amir, with a smile on his face and busy playing with a plastic cup in his hands, turned to Jill and said, "Do you know anything about Fibonacci sequence? What a crazy question! You clearly know. Let me explain the way my group was formed; it was something like the Fibonacci sequence. First, the numbers are small and don't seem very big, but the point is right here. In the Fibonacci sequence, each number is found by adding up the two numbers before it. Numbers increase considerably but not exponentially.

The same applies for 'Smokers!' The first steps were small ones, but the next steps were based on the two preceding ones and turned out to be much larger! I mean, maybe the coffee shop I set on fire seemed very small compared to the operations we performed later, but it was more difficult because it was among the first steps. Regarding the 300 Dollars I gave to Mike as the so-called 'tall man,' it was more difficult than inviting the former member of the army, though it doesn't seem logical.

The time I gave Mike the money, I had no notable credit and was somehow comparable to the prime numbers in the Fibonacci sequence. But as I took the small first steps and got the required credits, I dared to take larger steps while the possibility of our success had increased. On the other hand, for example, when I decided to add David in the group, I myself couldn't enter his life to invite him, but Adam, a committed member, could do it. The members of the group gained needed confidence from their friends who were members before them."

Jill looked at the nearly shredded plastic cup in Amir's hands and said, "Are you good at math?"

"No, but I'm over skilled in finding the relationships!" Amir answered.

Jill and Amir happened to start talking simultaneously but kept silent to let the other speak. After a short pause, Jill asked Amir to talk first. Amir said, "The way a reporter looks at me is different from the way people look at me here. Have you ever wondered if a man could feel himself falling if he is in absolute darkness? Perhaps he is ascending when the gravity is upward!

My story was the same. People saw that I was released, but they had no idea whether I was falling or ascending. They just knew that I had been separated from others. As I was not like them, I turned out to be the bad boy of the story. I did not even commit those things in wickedness. The most exciting part of the story was when I fell asleep while looking at Freddie Mercury's picture and felt like I was experiencing his feeling on the stage.

Thereafter, my enthusiasm and feeling became smaller. I even think that Freddie, after performing a few concerts, had lost his sense and performed as a habit just like me."

"Have you ever killed anybody and understand a killer's feeling as a result of doing so?" Jill asked.

Amir raised his shoulders and said, "No, but when I see the prisoners here and ask them about their feelings when committing a crime, they usually say that in their first few killings, they used to be stressed and excited, but those who have killed more than seven or eight people live with much unwillingness and seem to be indifferent towards life as if life has no color for them. They even don't enjoy killing a person anymore."

Jill closed her eyes, gulped her saliva, and said, "I think we should carry on with the story. Let's not tarnish the image too much!" Amir slightly threw the shreds of the plastic cup off the table and continued his account...

In the story ...

When I woke up every morning, I used to be so calm and relaxed. As Rolla was a small city, I had a feeling that the news of those two incidents would have already spread everywhere, but I really didn't expect such a reaction from the people. I don't know why, but I didn't fear anyone seeing me at the scene of the incident.

Nevertheless, I went out less on holidays and spent more time at home with family. Even my relationship with the family had gotten better. As I didn't need to move from Rolla to become famous, the whole city was talking about me. I had no more reason to be upset with my family. Our relationship had become normal as before.

The holidays finished at last, and I went to school. On the third day of school, something happened I never expected. Sheriff John Barr came to our school! The principal asked a few of the students and I to go to the school office. The Sheriff was a tall, heavyset man with blue eyes and a bald head and always had a smile on his face. We were all waiting at the school office without knowing why, then Susan entered. She tried to not make eye contact with any of us.

I never had that much anxiety at any time in my life. I could almost guess the whole story. In his investigations about the fire in the coffee shop, the sheriff had certainly noticed my sprayed warnings on the back wall and the drinks spilled over the floor. Susan, too, had exposed the guys who were informed of the story. A few days before the incident, I had talked to her about it; this automatically made me a suspect!

I was afraid of all those summoned to the school office

because they could cause danger for me, but I ignored the only one who was present there and truly a threat. However, it was a little late to regret what I had done. The Sheriff asked us to go out of the school office and individually return so we could talk to him.

It was Susan's turn first. We were waiting behind the door. All the boys seemed panicked and kept talking to each other. They were all afraid of the possible discipline they had to suffer because of drinking alcohol. I tried to show myself more relaxed than the rest, though I could face greater consequences in the end. My story could get me in trouble if the police traced me. I wished to be part of their circle, but suddenly, *he* returned to me and gave me my required self-confidence.

I really needed him more than anyone else. I was happy to see him again because I felt much less afraid. I had to think of what to say when I was interrogated by the sheriff. I was the third one who went inside the room. Still, four other boys were waiting in the queue. As I entered, John Barr looked at me with his usual smile and asked me to sit in the chair in front of him.

I knew if I wanted to playact those who knew nothing, the whole thing would get worse because Susan would have exposed everything beforehand. The sheriff asked me if I knew the reason I was there, and I said, "Yeah! Because my friends and I have bought alcohol drinks from a shop, when are still under legal age."

"Why did you do it? Except you, who else knew this, and how did you get in touch with them?" Barr asked.

"It's clear why! I just wanted to have some fun. All of those who knew about it are either waiting behind the door or have already talked to you! I don't drink alcohol, so I didn't have a direct link with them. I only knew that the guys were getting the drinks from somewhere, and as I didn't need alcohol, I never asked them about their connection." I answered in cold blood.

"If you don't drink, then why did you go to these places?" The sheriff asked in astonishment.

I, who was busy playing role, said, "Because they're my friends. I hate being alone, though I should not justify my wrongs."

"Why a mistake? You're saying you didn't drink alcohol!" Barr said.

"I had to report it much earlier! I could have stopped all these events and prevented further destructions." I replied.

"Which destructions? Do you mean the fire?" Barr said.

"Yeah! And the educational future of my friends and I, that we put in danger." I answered.

The sheriff secretively looked at me and said, "Do you know anything about the Smokers?"

"Yeah! It's the hottest news of the new year. So far all people are talking about them. Personally, it's been about a week since I've been informed about them and think there's a relation between them and the school. My reason to say this is because of what they afflicted on my school superintendent, Mr. Smith." I said.

I knew he would probably ask if there was any relationship between those two incidents that happened at our school. That was why I tried to sidestep him and raise that issue so that I could divert his attention and get off the list of suspects. Of course, with his secretive look and bitter smile, it was not easy for me to realize whether I made it or not.

However, he shook hands with me and thanked me for my cooperation. I got out the room and said nothing to anyone. On my way back home, Susan was the only one to expose me;

she came running toward me, trying to appease me. "Amir, I've no idea what you think about me, but It's not as it seems to be." She said.

I answered in a harsh tone, "I don't think about you anymore. By coming to me and trying to apologize, I am sure that it was your job. I just tried to help you the other day. It was my mistake, of course!"

I quickly passed by her. She called me by my name and said, "Amir, wait!"

I turned to her and said, "I wait for what? So that you say you're ashamed? If I were you, before talking about others, I would have talked about stealing and dispersing the drinks!"

As she wanted to continue her words, I interrupted her and went on my way home. I really didn't understand why she had to expose all of us. Was it just a slip of her tongue or a female ingratiation? Of course, it didn't matter. I learned the lesson that I shouldn't trust anybody outside the group. I didn't have enough time to look for the guilty. I had gotten addicted to my group, and I had to make it complete as long as the people were in shock and didn't know how to deal with the new phenomenon. The later I did it, the more difficult it would become because 'Smokers' was no longer unknown.

I returned home, and before doing my homework, I started to plan for our next missions. I decided to complete my notebook and start inviting new members. Taking for granted that Adam would have accepted our membership because of the favor I did for him, I already had three members—two of which had shown their honesty in advance.

Sam was the youngest member, and I had to keep him safe from the dangerous missions. The safest place to keep my book was at the Rolla public library. I remembered when I once had a research project and went to the library. There was a small corridor in the basement where they kept older books. I think even the owner of the library was not informed about the place!

It was very dark and covered with cobwebs around the corners. All over, the basement of the library was a little dusty. I remember when I touched a bookshelf: my fingertips were covered with dust. On the left side of the basement, there was a narrow hallway that seemed to be more intact. At the end of it, there were a few old wooden bookshelves with a dim light bulb shedding a little light on them. They could hardly be seen from the basement itself! It was more like the basement of a house in a horror movie!

I hid the book and the knife there in the last row of the bookshelves. I thought of assigning Sam as the person in charge of the library so that when our group members went there, they could initiate contact with him. Mike and Adam, too, would oversee making the situation ready for operations in a mission. If I was lucky to have David as the mastermind of the group, I would appoint him to sketch operational plans. For the rest of the members, I would assign some duty.

First, I had to officially register these four members! There were about two weeks left until the party that Adam's friend had talked about. So, I had to determine the duties of the other three members. I went to the library and asked about requirements for a job as librarian. A slim girl wearing thick eyeglasses and with a pony tail was at the counter. She politely answered that they wouldn't accept any further employees until the next summer. Upon my insistence, she showed me the weekly schedule, but she also said that two of the staff were due to leave the library until the summer. "No other way?" I asked.

"Unless one of our staff members isn't able to work, and we have no option but to recruit a substitute." She replied.

I went out of the library in despair. Just as I was exiting the gate and thinking about what to do, I stepped in a small pothole on the sidewalk in front of the library. I was lucky to prevent myself from falling. I had so much pain in my right ankle, but suddenly, a thought popped in my head. I totally forgot the pain! According to the library girl, if one couldn't work in there for any reason, there would be a vacancy for a new employee. The pothole was right in front of the library gate. Maybe that library girl had not noticed the pothole already! If, for any reason, I could do something to make her step in that pothole, maybe I could substitute Sam for her!

It was not the right thing to do, but according to Machiavelli, 'the ends justify the means!' I remembered the weekly schedule that she showed me. Some of the fields were highlighted with a marker; they were certainly her working hours. At the end of all the highlighted lines, I could see the closing time of 6:00 p.m.

I didn't have enough time for further planning. I had to make the group run before people's attention would be attracted by the 'Smokers!'

I looked at the pothole in front of the library gate. It was gray. Different ideas jumped in my mind, and I tried to choose the best. I just remembered that I had seen a handkerchief in our house cellar that we used for dusting. I quickly went back home, took it, and returned to the library. I shouldn't cover the pothole with it until six o'clock because it would hurt somebody else! I waited near the gate until 6:00 p.m. and looked through the window next to the gate to see the library girl and find out about her movement.

I had to cover the pothole with the handkerchief so that when she saw it, her unconscious mind wouldn't realize it. As soon as she would approach, I would quickly go to her and call her loudly so that her conscious mind, too, would be engaged with me and would totally forget about the pothole and step in it.

The aftermath was clear!

Right after my plan was fulfilled, I would tell Sam to proceed with getting a job at the library. That way, no one would suspect me for what will happen to the librarian. Although I had become terribly addicted to the 'Smokers' and did everything for it to remain, my conscience was in agony for the wickedness I was about to do. Anyway, I didn't have enough time to think about my conscience and the like.

The closer the time got to 6:00 p.m., the more doubtful I became. All my writings in the notebook happened to appear before my eyes, where I had complained about the injustices and inequalities, but I was about to commit an unjust and inhumane deed. It was the library girl's right to have her job. How in the world could I talk of light when a small piece of darkness was mixed with that light to build?! Even if I made it and could purify my city from impurity, that justice would be founded based on injustice and the violation of others' rights.

I was busy thinking about these things, and she got out of the gate right at 6:02. I was still in doubt. I told myself, "God damn it! I'll find another way." As she got closer to the pothole, I got closer to her. In the spur of the moment, I gave up my idea and while running toward her and calling her, I tried to draw her attention. She was about one meter from the pothole. I shouted, "Stop!" While scared, she froze. I removed the handkerchief and said, "Nothing! I just wanted to tell you mind the pothole here!"

She breathed deeply, and noticed that and thanked me, and said, "Thanks a lot! Oh by the way, today, you left early. I wanted to tell you that the library has a vacancy for a cleaning man. I wondered if you would like it."

I got surprised and said, "It's great. Tomorrow, I'll come to you, for sure. Of course, I am not looking for a job, but a friend of mine needs it. I'll inform him to come to you. Oh, sorry, I'm Amir. I should have introduced myself sooner!"

She, too, introduced herself: "I'm Sarah. Pleased to meet you. Yes. Please tell your friend to come to me when he wants to. Even if I'm not present, my colleague will certainly handle his request." She said goodbye and left.

I was so happy that on the one hand, I didn't do an inhumane thing; on the other, I got whatever I wished for. I was almost hopeless because I had not considered the case in which I was something other than a librarian. I tried to justify for myself that I was only fifteen by saying that it could be natural for a boy in my age to lack depth and have a limited vision.

I returned home and wrote in my notebook the duties of the four probable members in order of the letters of 'Smokers'. On a separate piece of paper, I told Sam to go to Sarah at the library and apply for a job as a janitor. I also wanted him, as the first member, to fingerprint a treaty of the group with his blood. I explained to him in his cigarette that whenever someone went to him asking for a cigarette, he had to say, 'Smoking is forbidden here.' If the person said, 'I don't smoke, but read the cigarette', it's the password, and Sam had to guide him to the hallway and do no more.

Sam's duty was to go where the book was hidden and pick up the cigarette-like papers. On Mondays, he had to go to the cemetery where the old beggar usually sat and put the papers in the left pocket of the beggar's coat. Right after that, he had to attach the sticker of the same alphabet letter on the back of the coat so members could know if they have a mission.

I also wrote the duties of the other three members—Mike, Adam and David—on the appropriate pages of the notebook, titled with the first letter of their names. The next morning trying not to attract anyone's attention, I hid some stickers of letters in my backpack. I then went to the basement of the library, passed by the hallway, and hid the things behind the

131

books in the last row of the bookshelves.

At midnight, I went to Sam's house and put a rolled paper with the letter 'S' on it behind his window. Sam was the first member. I didn't think that he wouldn't accept it. I wrote the same thing for Mike and put the letter 'M' on it. It was interesting that the first two letters of 'Smokers' matched the first letters of their names, but that was only by chance. Adam's first letter didn't match the third letter of 'Smokers!' So, I couldn't find a relation to prove to them they had been selected in advance. Doing so would make them crazy believers, though!

For Mike and Adam, I mentioned the way they had to connect with Sam and access the notebook. All other instructions and duties were already written in the notebook. The duties of Mike and Adam were hard to distinguish. They were both in charge of providing the means and conditions, and they had to take part in some missions, too. In all, they were enlisted manpower.

As David was considered an elite, I had assigned him to be the planner of the group. I didn't believe that he could afford operational missions, though it was not necessary. As before, I put Mike's fake cigarette inside an envelope and put it in front of his shop. I was almost sure that out of experience, he would realize the envelope belonged to him.

I used a cool trick for Adam. I would be waiting to see an old person who was not so careful of his or her surroundings to enter Adam's shop to have a drink. Then, a few steps before they went into the shop, I would get close to them and stick a piece of paper on their back. Adam, though, would probably notice the paper, and as soon as he wanted to tell them about it, he would see the phrase 'To Adam!' He would then understand that the paper is from the side of the 'Smokers.'

Of course, the risk was high. Maybe, everything wouldn't go

according to my plan, but I had risked so much during those days that I no longer was afraid. Mike, too, seemed to be smart enough to understand that he shouldn't consider the 'Smokers' as strangers! They had done him a great favor a few weeks ago! The mission I assigned to Adam was one in which he had to go to the students' party and do his best to invite David. Inside his fake cigarette, I had attached another piece of paper he had to pass to David.

The 'Smokers' had become so famous that they didn't need to be introduced in a small city like Rolla. Nearly everyone in the city knew who the 'Smokers' were looking for!

David had an unsuccessful suicide attempt, and it could be a sign of his despair in life. In the piece of paper, I tried to write some motivational advice to him. I mentioned that he was disappointed with this dirty world and had already made a suicide attempt but said that he should stand in front of it and fight instead of giving up and committing suicide.

I had heard that university students frequently commit suicide because of the hard courses that usually cause them to lose their motivation. I was hopeful that the 'Smokers' would give him enough motivation to feel that he had not been forgotten and that there were some people who needed him.

Later, I would ask Sam to go to the library and fingerprint his membership in his blood!

After doing these tasks on the day Adam was invited to the party, I attached the paper to the back of an old man who entered the coffee shop while making sure that nobody had noticed me. I then went back to my workplace and waited for the old man to leave the coffee shop. When I saw that the paper was not on his back, I realized that Adam had most likely gotten the paper.

It took about a week for the plans to come to fruition.

Everyone talked about 'Smokers.' At school, I noticed that some students were so impressed by 'Smokers' that they had formed a group with the same title! I wanted to see if they would accept me as a member, but their leader told me I didn't have enough potential to be efficient for the group! How would they react if they ever realized that I was the founder of the of the real group? I was no longer upset for not being seen, because I witnessed how seriously the people of the city were talking about the young boy that was never taken seriously!

Even thinking about it made me get goosebumps. I didn't want to stand still now. Before it got late, I had to accomplish the job. I knew that I had to go to the library to check the book and meet Sam and Sarah. It was weighing on my mind that I had to pretend I was Sam's friend.

I had to approach with Sam formally so that the rules of the group focused on not establishing a relationship between members would be observed. I had to go to the library when Sarah was finished with her work there—after 6:00 p.m. or before noon. In the meantime, it was interesting for me to see Sam's reaction, and I was also a little stressed that he wouldn't take the group so seriously when he saw me at the library. However, if he was really dedicated to the group, he should accept me when I said the password.

I also had to be careful not to agree or reject the offers as soon as I read them because it was impossible that the tall man would immediately check the book to see my answer. Since cellphones were not so common those days, it was also possible that in case I would answer right away, he would get suspicious of me and doubt if there ever was a 'tall man.' So, I had to wait for a day or for a few hours to go to the library to announce my final answer.

The good point was that because I had severely warned them against any connection out of the group, it was less probable that they would discuss their membership procedures and find a clue to reach to me as the one behind the curtain. However, nothing was determined yet.

A week after, I went to the library and found Sam there. First, he didn't think that I knew anything about the story, so he began talking about common things in a panic, but I abruptly asked him if he had a cigarette. He was stunned and swallowed his saliva. After a few seconds he answered nervously, "Smoking is forbidden here!"

"I'm not here to smoke a cigarette but to read it!" I said right away. His eyes were about to pop out his sockets. He said nothing, and I also did not. He just pointed to the basement with his finger, and I walked toward there. No one heard our conversation.

I saw three bloody fingerprints in the part of the notebook where members had to cut their fingers and put their markings. I was convinced about their true belief in the group. It was like a dream. I didn't have to wake up! I just had to continue the dream. During the past week, I had seen them sticking plasters on their fingers, but I couldn't be assured that they joined the group until I saw their fingerprints in the notebook.

A couple of days were left until the party, so I had to wait to see if David accepted our membership. The great thing was that all members had a very natural behavior at school and work. The sheriff didn't show up at school again. I wondered if I was still under his surveillance or if he had removed me off his suspects list. Anyway, I managed to do what I had to do!

We had become the main subject of all the media. The day of the party came at last. I knew the address of the party. It was a house in the vicinity of the campus, known as the place for students' parties. I had passed it several times. Wandering around the place, I kept watching to see if Adam would go there. He was one of the last guests to arrive.

I was not sure if I could enter the party. I waited for a short while but couldn't last waiting any longer and tried to go there. I was watching to see when a few guests went in or got out together so that I could enter the house among them. I made it at last. In fact, the party was so crowded that no one noticed me. There were alcoholic drinks on the tables, and young students were mostly busy smoking cigarettes.

I looked for Adam among the guests. I found him asking about David. The guy pointed to a room, and Adam made his way to it. I followed him, too. I had already seen David's picture in a local newspaper. He was too slim. His face clearly showed that he was addicted to narcotics. He was sitting in a sofa and was busy smoking. Adam sat beside him. They talked a little bit with each other, and Adam went to the half-opened door to close it.

He shouldn't see me at all. I tried to find some place to hide and found the bathroom. I went toward it and found it locked from behind. As I was pressing down the doorknob, it opened and a young boy and girl with drowsy eyes got out. I couldn't tell if they were drunk or high. As the girl was passing by, she pinched my cheek and said, "I didn't know that kids stay awake until this time of night!" She smiled coquettishly and went to a corner.

I don't know why, but my face turned a little red! For a moment, I totally forgot why I was there! Another guy in the party saw the girl and approached her. Just as I was going into the bathroom, I heard the girl saying to the guy, "Doesn't it cause trouble for you to let kids attend the party?" He asked, "which kid?"

Dammit! It couldn't be worse. I didn't wait for the girl to point at me, and I quickly went toward the party. Among the crowd, I luckily found the exit door behind the house and made my way toward it. I knew it was impossible for me to enter the house again. Maybe I didn't need to go there at all. Anyway,

Adam was with David, so everything would likely go well. However, I really couldn't stop my curiosity.

I reviewed the house's plan in my mind to find out the location of the window of that room. I got it. It was opposite of where I stood. I went toward the wall where the window was. Luckily, it was open. Since it was quiet outside, I could almost hear their conversation. Adam was busy talking about something. In his answers, David kept hinting that he was uncertain of his current situation. It was clear that he was not willing to join.

Ultimately, David said, "I'm fed up. What are you saying? I just want to enjoy the party. Now that a few kids have written some nonsense on a wall, there's no reason to believe anything!"

"No kids are involved. The one behind the story has saved my life. He knows everything and has pals everywhere. You won't believe it if I tell you how he invited me with a piece of paper attached to the back of an old man!" Adam said.

"Wait! You say they're everywhere. OK. Tell him to come talk to me," David said quickly.

"Not this way! Trust me, David!" Adam said.

David laughed and said, "I don't even trust myself anymore! What're you talking about?" That moment, somebody called them from outside the room and asked them to step inside the hall.

"Our discussion is not finished yet. We will return and talk more," Adam said.

"I told you to tell him to come and talk with me," David said.

Their voices faded out, and I knew they had left the room. On the one hand, I was happy to see that I was believable for Adam. On the other, I was upset that David didn't believe

Adam and turned a deaf ear to my story. In the meantime, I was not sure if Adam gave David my written message early at the party.

I was busy thinking about these, and I accidentally touched my jacket's pocket and sensed something inside it. There was the note slip and the pen I used the other day at school. I repeated to myself that I always had to have those notes and pen because they would be useful in such times. As *he* had totally infiltrated within me, I was waiting for pure ideas to jump in my mind at any moment.

Yeah! I had to write something on the note slip and throw it in the room from the window so that they would believe 'Smokers' were present everywhere. So, I wrote the following, "David! We are present everywhere! You don't need to give up anymore. We will grant you bigger goals in life than school, partying, and daily routines." I rolled the paper like cigarette and threw it in the room.

A few minutes later, they returned to the same room. They were still discussing the issue. Adam insisted, and David rejected. As they were busy talking, David shouted, "Who has dropped his cigarette on my bed?" I realized he had seen the paper.

"Oh, my God! It's not a cigarette. It's a note from the tall man!" Adam said.

"Is it a game or a joke? You want to fool me. I know it's your trick!" David said.

Adam swore he didn't do it. "David, you wanted him to give you a message. Here it is! You better know I never lied to you. How in the world did I know that our conversation would go on like this?! The whole time, I have been within your view. You know me!" Adam said.

It seemed that David had read the message. "Let me see where he is!" David said. I got to know that he intended to look at the window from outside the house because when they got out the room, I heard the door being shut. They also knew that the message could have been thrown in the room only from the window. I immediately started to run away. Suddenly, I saw them again! The Damned ones! The very young mute boy with his dog, staring at me again!

How in the world were they doing this at this time of the night? Why did they always appear before me at the most sensitive moments? I hated them. I had a feeling that the young boy was the angel of death and was after me to catch my soul. Even Hot Coffee was not near there so I would guess his house was in the vicinity. Anyway, I didn't have time to think about these Q and A questions. I just had to run away. I ran as fast as I could and hid behind a church at the opposite side of the street.

I couldn't hear their voices anymore. My staying there just increased the danger of being exposed. Without looking back, I just started to run toward home. When I got home, I climbed the wall to reach my room's window. This was the way I usually returned inside my room at late night, whenever I was late at nights and I didn't want my family to know about it. I remembered the first time '*he*' insistently asked me to jump down from my room's window. I think *he* saw these days in advance, that *he* made such weird requests! Anyway, I was in my room. I couldn't sleep almost the whole night. Everything was fifty-fifty.

I just had to wait. Two days past and the only way for me to get sure if David had believed the story was to go to the library. I went there and saw Sam who even didn't show any reaction by seeing me. Sarah was also there. She was about to say hello to me, but I was so busy thinking about David that I passed her by. I behaved so normally and continued my way toward the basement.

I opened the book and saw the fourth bloody fingerprint. I was so happy and excited that I wanted to shout, but I couldn't. As soon as I closed the book, I saw a note laid next to it. It read, "I hope it's all real and turns to be good for me to change the hateful way of my life. I have nothing to lose. Maybe this group is what I'm looking for, though I'm still doubtful about it—your handwriting is different from the one in the book! I am not sure if that was you or someone else."

Oh, my God! I was in a hurry the night I wrote the note to David, so it didn't match the previous handwriting that I had practiced so much. The handwriting on the note was my usual handwriting and could expose me, though it was less probable that David could guess my handwriting because we had never met each other before. I was also worried that Sam's curiosity would drive him to see the note and identify me if he ever remembered my handwriting.

I felt relieved when I opened the note slip because I understood that it hadn't been opened before. David's duty was to go to the library on Wednesdays to learn about his mission, if any. Then he had to make plans and write the duties of each member in their separate notes, rolled the papers and put them beside the book.

Sam, too, had to check the place after David left and take the rolled papers. On Mondays, early in the morning, he had to go to the cemetery and put the fake cigarettes in pocket of the old beggar for the members to pick them and get ready for the mission. Frankly, I was a little worried that David's doubt would make him wait to see the 'tall man' who would go toward the book. But David wouldn't leave the message there if he ever intended to do so.

BURN FOR GOOD

I shouldn't stop. The only way to keep their trust was to continue the game I had already begun. The excitement among people about the 'Smokers' had faded a little. I thought it was time to assay the group in a real way. So, I tried to look for a pretext to begin a mission involving all the members together. I had a difficult job to do.

First, considering that the two previous incidents in the city were directly connected with the school issues, I shouldn't plan the new mission related to the school or university because the people would probably suspect that 'Smokers' was a school-based group. Secondly, I didn't want anyone thinking that the happenings were a child's play. On the other hand, If I planned to make any action regarding the more important issues of society, the police would already have those subjects under surveillance in advance.

What made it difficult was the fact that because it had to be such a considerable mission, the people would believe a real group was involved. In the meantime, the mission had to be concealed from police. To find a reason for the mission, I began reading the incident pages of the newspapers, watching TV news programs, and listening to the daily talking of the people to find out what they were complaining about.

My other problem was that I was a fifteen-year-old boy with no detective training to apply in my plans. So, I began reading a detective novel to gain the vision.

Sometimes, I chose some subjects from the newspapers, but they seemed to be much beyond the potential of our group in terms of operational or detective aspects, and we also lacked access to the required information to be able to get involved in a mission. Of course, there were some missions we could handle, but they were more suitable for cities around Rolla, like Springfield, Salem, or St. Louis.

For instance, one of the strange incidents that used to happen in the surrounding cities was that every now and then, people would steal their own money and valuables or leave their homes while wearing their night gowns or pajamas. Those who witnessed these strange behaviors called the police.

According to the reports, they didn't realize the police at first; however, as soon as police managed to arrest them, they were shocked to find themselves in that situation in the middle of streets at midnight. The reports said that none of those people ever remembered the reason for their deeds. When I saw their pictures in local newspapers, I noticed that they belonged to no certain class or age group.

Some of them carried their own money or jewelry, and since there were no plaintiffs, they were released. There were some reasons behind such similar strange behaviors in different cities around, but because such cases didn't happen in Rolla, I didn't pay much attention to them.

It's true that there were occasional thefts in Rolla, but there were no reports of hypnotic people wandering in the streets at midnight, and it was not only the money or valuables that were stolen. So, there couldn't be any connection between the upcoming incidents and the thefts. That's why it didn't matter to me.

After a substantial amount of consideration, the result was disappointing. I couldn't find any noticeable subject to make plans for the missions. All over, Rolla was a quiet city. I once read in a newspaper that a few people robbed a gas station and stole only a small amount of money. I didn't want to start the first collective mission of the group like that, but I had to plan a mission so that the members would be confident and trust its real nature.

I had to go to the library and write about the not-so-striking idea in the part of the missions of the notebook so that David would start making plans. He didn't believe wholeheartedly in the group, and I had to propose an eye-catching pre-plan for him, but I had failed to find a suitable one. What should I do?

I decided to handle the case through Sam. I would give him a paper of the mission, and he would hand it to David. I really didn't know the reason. Maybe, that way Sam would feel he had a special position in the group. I admit it wasn't a good idea, but it was the best one that jumped in my mind.

As usual, I jumped out of my window at midnight and headed toward Sam's home to put the message behind his window. As I was riding my bike, I saw a man getting out of a supermarket in a strange manner. It wasn't an around-the-clock supermarket. First, I thought he was the shop owner. I had already purchased items from that supermarket and knew the shop owner. Anyway, I shouldn't be seen. I waited undercover until he got closer so I could see his face.

He was not the owner of the supermarket. His mysterious

behavior and continuous looking around made me suspicious of him. He got on his motorbike. I suspected he probably was the one who stole from the gas station, so I began to chase him on my bike. I was about to lose him, but he had stopped only three blocks further.

I got off the bike and did my best to get closer to him so I could identify him. He went to the door of a house and knocked very gently on it. A young boy opened the door. I was sure I had already seen him somewhere. I could hardly focus at that time of the night, but I did! It was not too long since I saw him at the college's party. He was the same boy who was with the girl that pinched my cheek. I had seen them at the party, getting out of the bathroom together.

I could hear their conversation almost clearly. The man said to the young boy in a harsh voice, "This is the last time I'm doing this for you. I told you before: If you want it, you have to tell me a few days earlier."

"Yeah! I know, dude. I'm not feeling good at all," the young boy said.

"First, money!" The man said.

"Sure! Here—all for you. Just give me that shit! Hurry up," the young boy said.

The boy took out some money from his pocket, gave it to the man, and took the black bag. The man got on his bike and disappeared quickly. The young boy, with his face as white as a ghost, closed the door. It was almost clear from the time of the night that there was no alcohol or cigarettes inside the bag!

The man had left, and I didn't know the guy I saw at the party. What should I do? Suddenly, a light in my brain lit up! I didn't know him, but I knew someone who knew him!

I changed my mind to give the paper of the mission to Sam

and returned home. I was busy thinking about that supermarket. What could be offered in a supermarket that a person would be so eager to get at midnight? First, I thought that it was because the young boy was under legal age and feared to be punished by 'Smokers!' However, when I thought about it, I gathered that we were not much validated yet.

So, what could be inside the shop? It was not so difficult to guess. The first thing could be the drug. How in the world could drug be found in a supermarket? I thought about it the whole night. The next morning, I went to the supermarket on the pretext of buying some snacks. Everything seemed normal. The man riding the motorbike was not there. As I was busy looking around the shelves, I happened to hear a customer asking the owner of the shop if they had any olive oil. The owner, an old man with grey hair and big glasses, said that he had to look in the warehouse to see if any were left.

I got out of the shop without buying anything. I had found the answer! Whatever it was, it should be found in the warehouse. I had gotten the idea at last! I went back home and began planning for the new mission! I made the plan in such a way that David—who knew the young boy receiving the black bag because they happened to be at the same students' party—had to try to befriend him and gradually built his trust, then ask him for some drugs.

Since David had once attempted suicide and was almost addicted to cigarettes and alcohols, no one would suspect him to be bluffing. When he could build trust, he would ask the young boy to link him with the drug dealer. I got to know from their conversation that because the young boy had been late to order, the drug dealer was forced to go to the supermarket at midnight to supply the stuff.

Later, David would place an untimely order for drugs so that the drug dealer would be compelled to go to the supermarket. Then, as soon as he went in, Mike and Adam would enter and

145

trap him inside the shop. Right after that, they would stun him by blows to the head and go inside the storeroom to make sure the drugs are there. At last, they would set the supermarket, not the storeroom, on fire so that the police could detect the drugs inside the building. Before leaving the shop, Mike and Adam would leave the message of 'Smokers' by spraying it on the wall. This way, 'Smokers' would formally announce itself to the city. During almost all missions, I couldn't see what was going on in detail because I was mostly an observer from the outside.

Since it was winter and would likely snow, the shoe prints of members could be traced by the police. In the meantime, the supermarket was equipped with closed circuit cameras. So, I went to Walmart and bought three masks and three pairs of boots for the members to utilize on their missions. I later went to the library, hid them in the dark and dusty bookshelf, and ordered the members to pick up their items. Since that day was not very quiet, I was not at the center of attention, so no one noticed me with the bag of supplies.

The masks were the remaining Halloween masks from the year before. They were black Mickey Mouse faces with circular ears, red eyes, and sharp white teeth. I left 200 Dollars for David so that he wouldn't spend his own money on drugs during the mission.

In the missions' part of the notebook, I ordered them to bring along as much money they could so it could later be divided between them. They also had to put the money in their pockets so that when the police checked the cameras, they wouldn't realize that any money had been taken out of the shop. By the way, it was illegal money and couldn't be tracked.

I owed all these experiences to the movies I had already seen and to *his* brilliant ideas! I was not myself and had found a new character!

146

David went to the library, read his mission, took his things, wrote the missions in the fake cigarettes, rolled them, and put them in the bookshelf. Sam, too, put the fake cigarettes in the pocket of the old beggar and attached the stickers at the back of the beggar's coat for Adam and Mike to be informed about their duties.

Since the mission had to start at midnight, we were not worried about being seen. It seemed that David had made the plan in a way that after he drew the young boy's confidence, he could attach a sticker at the back of the beggar's coat so Mike and Adam would know that they had to be prepared for midnight. They both had to go to the cemetery every day to find the details of their mission.

David had already written all the details on the fake cigarettes for Mike and Adam. I knew nothing about the details, as I had not read them. After the mission, I got to know that one of Mike's duties was to supply the fuel. I even didn't know exactly what kind of drugs they sold. It was after the completion of the mission that I read about it in the notebook.

Mike had forgotten to pick up his boots. I went to the library every day to see the boots being picked up, so I guess it was the day of the mission.

I had guessed right. After a week, when I noticed there were no boots and masks, I understood it was the day of the mission. During that week David probably built his friendship with the young addicted man to get drug dealer address. I had no idea about the time of the mission and could not ask anyone.

I hid around the place until two past midnight. I waited there for about an hour. It was cold, and I was hungry. I saw Mike and Adam waiting for the dealer behind a building across street. Because my location was higher than them, it was easier for me to recognize them. At last, the man riding the motorbike appeared. As soon as he entered the supermarket, Mike and Adam blindsided him and got into the shop.

I could never imagine them being so serious and harsh when they blew the man a few times in the face and even didn't let him shout. They all got in the supermarket. My heart was restless. I felt like going inside the shop and sharing the mission, but I knew everything would be spoiled. I looked around to see if anyone else was there—not a living soul!

A few minutes later, I heard the sound of a burning fire. All at once, the three men got out the supermarket. The face of the bike-riding man was bloody, and he seemed whacked. Mike and Adam dropped him on the ground, sprayed something below his feet, and quickly ran away.

I couldn't see the words they sprayed. In less than a minute, the sound of people crying for help to extinguish the fire could be heard, and I knew that any moment fire men would be there. I immediately returned home and did not even look behind to see if anyone saw me or not.

Along the way, I heard the sound of fire truck sirens. I went inside an alley and waited for the truck to pass by the street. Then, I continued my way back home.

The whole night, I was thinking how could I have made such different characters from two ordinary guys who I never imagined to be so violent. Thereafter, I happened to realize how religious missionaries managed to control the people by inspiring them and creating a charismatic personality.

I was sure that the next day, the people of the city would talk about the 'Smokers.' David, too, who clearly had trusted the group, proved how effective he could be.

MYSTERIOUS CIRCUS

I had a feeling that I had conquered the world. With a sense of joy and excitement, I fell into a deep sleep. The next day, as I predicted, the people of the city were talking about us. Though the mission was done at midnight, everyone at school was informed about it the same morning. I also saw a picture in a local newspaper that the drug dealer had fainted on the ground where a warning was. It said, "We clean up the city from drugs!" Above his head was 'Smokers.' I understood that the storeroom of the supermarket was actually a lab to produce crystal meth. I tried to show myself excited and listened more than I talked. The school kids talked exaggeratedly about the incident. One of them quoted his father as saying that the 'Smokers' group has been founded by an American senator and will make its activity public in the whole country soon.

Sam was behaving so naturally that I tried to imitate him when I got carried away. His behavior made him seem older than his age. We exchanged smiles when we saw each other among the crowd of the school kids.

149

We were both defeated before, but now we were both satisfied and successful, of course. We knew that the whole thing would go well if we kept it a secret.

After school, I saw the newspapers and the people who were frantically talking about 'Smokers.' I had shocked the quiet and silent city—but not so silent! I previously thought that Rolla was a hushed city, but during the mission, I realized that it had hidden public outcries. If it was not hidden, many people would have noticed it long ago. I did not have any fear, and I did not think about any unpleasant probable incidents in the future.

I had already decided to run away from Rolla and move to my dream city, but now I was satisfied because I was turning Rolla into my dream city. Where I saw or read the word 'Smokers,' I substituted my own name in.

On my way to work, I heard a guy telling his friend that last midnight, he had seen someone running in the street. Maybe he was lying, trying to spread rumors.

Rolla is a small city with small alleyways. Even if no one could have identified Mike and Adam last night, it was possible that in our next missions, we would be seen and stopped by someone. I had to make a fool-proof plan. We had to do the next mission with a car so that we could leave the place immediately without any risk of being identified. What that guy said made me think of a new member for the group.

I couldn't assign this duty to Mike and Adam, because their responsibilities were assigned before, and I shouldn't behave in such a way that would cause people to doubt the capabilities of the group and think that we were not strong enough to recruit a driver! I saw Mike and Adam in their workplace and noticed how naturally they behaved with each other and with the people, and frankly, I doubted for a moment if they were involved in the mission last night at the supermarket!

After finishing my work, I went to the library to pick up the moneys. Everything seemed normal. I made my way toward the bookshelf where the bag of money was hidden; that part of the library seemed as if it was out of access to the patrons, because I still could see the cobwebs covering some of the bookshelves.

Luckily, the bookshelf where I had hidden my notebook had almost no clientele. The bag of moneys was heavy. I put the moneys inside my backpack and went out of the library. Just as I got out of the gate, Sarah called me. For a moment, I was glued, wondering what she wanted to tell me. Maybe she had wondered why I continuously went to the basement of the library and realized the whole story! In that case, no money would remain at the bookshelf for me to pick up!

In the meantime, it occurred to me that, maybe, all these were a trap by police to identify me. What was the police car doing in front of the library? Surely, they were waiting for me to get out there and arrest me. Sarah was repeatedly calling me while I was deep in thought. I turned and said, "Yeah?"

"Sorry, Mr. Shahri! I think it's time you extend your membership," Sarah said.

Oh my God! For a moment I felt thunderstruck! I became so happy and said, "Yeah, yeah, sure!" I stretched my hand to the backpack to pick some money for membership. Once I unzipped the backpack, I froze. If Sarah happened to see how much money I had with me, she would surely report me to the police. I looked at her eyes to find out if she had seen it. Luckily, she didn't seem to have realized.

I took my wallet and quickly zipped my backpack. I paid Sarah my charge for the membership. She thanked me, and I took a deep breath while getting out there. Sam was busy cleaning; all this time, I did not know if he thought I was the 'tall man' or his right-hand. By the way, he believed everything so much that he did not bother doubting.

I returned home, locked the door to my room, and began counting the moneys. Oh, my God! One hundred thousand Dollars! The damned bucks we gained by a simple move! That's it. I just had to give a little motivation to the members of the group.

Maybe, Mike and Adam had picked some of the moneys for themselves, but it was important that they had returned one hundred thousand. It was a sign that they had gained enough belief in 'Smokers!'

I had to take some of the money for myself so that Sam wouldn't doubt I was the boss of the 'Smokers.' I returned 20,000 Dollars to the library and wrote the amount each member could take.

Sam put the fake cigarettes inside the pocket of the beggar's coat, notifying the other three to pick their shares. He picked his share, too. It was cool that Sam had changed his glasses. I kept the rest of the money under my bed for a rainy day.

A few days passed. The city was almost quiet, but again, there was the news about coming of a circus to the city. I already had heard about it at school, and it was always interesting for me to see the clowns. Apart from our hidden activities, I just wanted to spend my normal life and enjoy occasions like a circus show.

Many of the school kids brought the brochures of the 'Fun Time' circus to school and got excited when talking about the events of the show. I took one of the brochures on the ground and read it. The circus acts included clowns, magicians, jugglers, tightrope walkers, trained elephants, and a skillful knife thrower. They had a sideshow, too.

The circus also had a special program that people could go to and take photos with the performers. The circus had its own team of photographers, with some of their selected photos printed in the brochure. Oh, my God! One of the persons in a photo looked very familiar to me. I was sure I had seen him somewhere before. As much as I thought, I couldn't remember anything.

I took the brochure home with me and put it on the table in my room. Two days later, before doing my homework, I decided to tidy up my room. While I was putting my newspapers and other things on the table, I happened to see something I never thought of! The brochure of the 'Fun Time' circus was among the newspapers that I used to read for making our missions.

Part of a newspaper had a photo on it and stuck out from under the brochure. The other photo printed on the brochure shared something interesting. In the news photo, one of those hypnotic-like people who brought along their valuables and wandered in the streets at midnight resembled a guy who had taken a photo with the Fun Time clowns. The two photos happened to be placed side by side and made it easy for me to identify the guy.

It couldn't be accidental. I didn't pay attention to it before because it didn't have anything to do with Rolla, but now that the circus was about to come to our city, I couldn't ignore it.

I went to the library, and in the missions' chapter of the book, I assigned David to find out if there were any relationship between the thefts outside the city and the group of clowns. I had heard that David was a computer genius, so he could certainly do research to see if he could find a clue.

It was risky that I asked him to do the job because the members would possibly think that I knew everything in advance. So, I made the request as if I was informed about the news, and I had asked David to do it because all other members were kept in the informed about every mission. This way, I could draw his confidence more.

It took a few days for David to return with an interesting answer: Fun Time circus entered the city a day earlier to meet the people, would stay one more day after finishing their show, and later leave the city. Their alleged reason was to have an excursion in the city.

There was something odd. Those hypnotic people wandering in the streets were found the same night the circus left the city! Until then, of course, no report on any relationship was issued, and I was not even sure if any research had been made about it.

The more unusual thing was that it didn't happen in all the cities they performed the show, but it occurred in every other city! To be more precise, nothing weird happened in Saint Charles, where they had a previous show, but in their next stop at Chesterfield, the same thing had happened. Their next show in Cuba, Wisconsin entailed no such incident, and their next destination was Rolla! So, there was a possibility that we would witness the mysterious account.

David thought that there was magic in such a way that in the day of the show, people were enchanted to steal gold for the circus people. Anyway, I had gotten a new idea that was worth trying for a new mission.

I made the plan. Since a lot of people attended the circus show, it was not reasonable to ask the group members to wear their masks. So, I ordered them to get tickets and enter the circus in a normal way and watch the circus people once they arrived in the city a day earlier than the show for the people to visit them. They also had to keep watching them until the last moment of their exit so that they could see any incidents.

Mike and Adam had to be around with their fake cigarettes on their lips and not light them. Once any one of them would notice something unusual, he had to throw his cigarette on the ground so that the other members got alarmed. Mike, too, had to take a spray bottle and a baseball bat and hide them in a place near the circus building a day before the show and utilize them in case he recognized the thief and could find the place where the jewels and valuables were hidden if that is the case. The police had already failed to stop the individuals responsible for the theft!

Mike had to later knock the thief unconscious with the bat without leaving any trace and would spray the word 'Smokers' behind the circus tent. Adam, too, would set a part of the circus tent on fire so that people would leave. This way, police would recognize the place of the jewelries and valuables and would return them to the owners in other cities, and the 'Smokers' would prove to be the saviors of the people. Since I was not with members all the time, they likely talked together. Who knows maybe Adam and David already talked about missions or the tall man, but since I did not want to mess with the group, I did not snoop inside the group.

However, people's visits with the circus performers on the first day went on normally. I was around the place to watch things from a close. I didn't notice anything doubtful like hiding the people or hypnotizing them. The only thing that looked somewhat unusual was that when the magician took a photo with anyone, he put one of his hands around their neck and held the magic ball in his bosom.

Sometimes, he shook hands with them, and after a short pause, he bid them goodbye! I thought to myself that he had maybe not been a native English speaker and that he repeatedly said the same things because of this. Anyway, I didn't get anything special that day.

The day of the show arrived. I went to the circus together with my family. I continually watched Mike and Adam to see if they had the fake cigarettes on their lips to figure out if everything was alright. Sam was there, too. He was a little shocked to see me. Many of the school kids, the personnel, and the school

AMIRHOSSEIN SHAHRI

janitors were attending the show.

My angle with Mike and Adam to the vertical axis of the tent was about 120 degrees, so I had no problem seeing them. They never noticed me the day I came in one after the other and sat on their seats. Everything looked normal. The clowns and the tightrope walker performed their acts. The clowns seemed somehow suspicious. They stared too much at the people. Mike got out the circus tent to watch from outside.

According to the circus schedule, it was the turn of the trained elephants to show off, but to my surprise, the magician arrived at the scene. He announced that if anyone would be a volunteer to go to the scene and let the magician disclose his or her personal information, they would be permitted to have a free ride of the elephant. Well, the kids raised their hands since they had nothing special to hide!

All Adam's attention was focused on the exit door at the side of the tent, where Mike went out from. The magician chose a few of the volunteers and disclosed things about them like their names and date of birth and even told what they had in their pockets. While the audience had their eyes on the magician, Mike came in with no cigarette on his lips and stared at Adam!

It was a sign for Adam to start his job. Mike went out again. Adam stood up and made his way to the exit door at the other side of the tent. I was sure that sooner or later, everything would be mixed up. Sam, who was already informed about the mission, pretended to be nauseous and left with his family.

A real firework was about to begin! I started reverse counting. While the magician was talking to the volunteers, an elephant rushed to the scene. The clowns followed the animal. This meant that the coming of the elephant at that time was off schedule.

156

Suddenly, someone shouting 'fire' was heard from a corner. A panic began. The fire outside the circus building was not big enough to affect the tent. People were frantically running out the circus. In less than two minutes, the firefighters and the police arrived.

My parents called me loudly to not to stop there and go along with them. The fire had started from the cage where they kept the elephant. That was why the animal rushed to the scene. I wondered why Adam had chosen that place to set ablaze. Maybe it was not his job. Anyway, I couldn't stay there, as they might suspect me.

I returned home and behaved normally. Two days later, I went to the library to read the chapter of 'Mission Description' in the notebook. It was mentioned in there that when Mike got out the circus, he chased two of the clowns making their way toward the woods, where a small cabin was built among the trees and seemed to belong to the circus.

The pavilion was painted in green, red, and white stripes—the same colors used by the Fun Time circus and of course my national flag. Mike had questioned why the pavilion was not set up beside other circus buildings. So, he chased them to the pavilion and happened to see that a lot of money and jewelries were hidden inside the pavilion. He had entered quickly, and before the clowns turned their heads to see him, he stunned them with blows on their heads with the baseball bat.

Then, he sprayed the word 'Smokers' behind the cabin and returned to the circus to signal Adam. Adam, too, started to pour gasoline onto the circus tent and continued pouring it until the tank was empty.

They immediately set the gas on fire, and the flames covered the whole path until it reached the cage of the elephant. As the cage was not locked, the scared animal ran away and entered the scene. Those who were busy smoking or eating outside the tent noticed the fire and began to shout for help.

Well, I understood details of the mission. Now I had to see the people's reaction. A few days later, I read in the newspapers that the police had recognized the hiding place of the moneys and jewelries through 'Smokers' and had inquired about the stolen things, then returned them to their owners living in the surrounding cities.

This way, the 'Smokers' had gained name and fame even at a small town like Rolla. It was good news, but the bad news was that a boy called Thomas had gotten lost in the commotion. The weird thing was that no relationship was found between his disappearance and the circus. It was true that the circus people had been arrested on charges of theft, but the police had not found any document against them in regard with kidnapping.

Thomas was not among those who took photos with the magician or volunteered. It looked as if his getting lost had nothing to do with the Fun Time. In fact, in other cities, there were only reports about the theft of money and valuables, not kidnapping.

According to confessions by the magician, he claimed to have had a supernatural power and could access the personal details of people by touching their bodies. He also said that he enchanted them by the violet magic ball in no time. That was why, according to him, they stayed in the city one more day after the show was finished; he said that the enchanted people would bring along their moneys and valuables for him and forget that they had done so!

It was more like Harry Potter than reality! If anyone ever had such a power, why did he have to do such a wretched thing when he could benefit many? Well, it's no reason that if someone has a supernatural power, he also has the sense to utilize it for his well-being. However, it was bad news. We had done what was right, and Thomas getting lost was an incident that could have happened anyway.

TWO CHURCHES

I waited for a few weeks and stopped the operations so that the city would become quiet again. Then, I would start finding new members. Weeks passed until I gathered it was the time to recruit new members.

I was looking for a new member that I saw Jacob's family at school. We were summoned to the school office again. I had no idea why I had to go there. Cody and Henry were there, too. So, it surely had something to do with Jacob! Sheriff Barr was also there. We both got surprised upon seeing each other. We exchanged a cold hello and were called one-by-one to the room.

The principal explained that it had been two days since Jacob disappeared. I felt so ecstatic about our reflection that I paid no attention to what happened around me. That was why I hadn't realized Jacob's absence. Henry, Cody, and Jacob's family talked about his weird words and deeds before his disappearing.

The last time he was seen at school, he had been busy studying his lessons with a classmate. So, he had stayed longer at school but never returned home. In fact, since the time I was engaged with the 'Smokers,' I didn't spend my time with Jacob and his pals. Seemingly, Jacob had told Henry that he would go where his words would be heard and where someone would understand him. According to the principal, Jacob had a cold relationship with his family due to his spiritual problems.

"It's interesting; we're meeting again!" The sheriff said.

"But, it's not interesting for me at all," I replied.

The sheriff changed his tone and said, "No, no! I didn't mean it. There's no reason to be afraid of me. I'm here just to help."

"I fear no one! However, every time I see you here, I feel like something bad has happened!" I said.

The sheriff raised his shoulders and said, "Well, my job demands that I handle bad happenings!"

I answered in almost a harsh tone, "Then, please do your job! My friend is lost, and you are asking me about him. If I knew where he was, I would certainly tell."

The principal, who seemed to be upset by my unpleasant tone, wanted to make me quiet, but the sheriff pointed with his hand to stop him and said, "Yes. If you remembered anything, let us be informed. I won't bother you more." I bowed my head and left the room. I even didn't talk to Henry or Cody.

I was very upset because I knew what Jacob was talking about. He possibly had believed my story and had gone to the same place I took them that night and probably got lost. I had to go there and check. After I finished my job, I went there.

Along the way, I had a feeling that someone was chasing me. I reached the dirt road at last. As I was moving forward, I happened to see the same tree on which a sign was engraved. Once again, I went near the tree and started searching around, and all of the sudden, a small thing on the ground drew my attention. I got closer.

Jacob's key ring was there which had a small flashlight. I knew it was his. It was a difficult situation. If I informed the police, they would inquire about why he was there and would ultimately realize that I had been, wittingly or unwittingly, behind that happening. Next, Sam would also notice that all these events were fabricated and possibly expose me. I couldn't ruin it all now that everything was happening perfectly. If I was the cause of this incident, I had to fix it.

I picked up the key ring and quickly left the place so that I could think about what to do next. I wondered if Jacob's getting lost had to do anything with that sign on the tree. I couldn't let things be ruined. I was finally experiencing an enjoyable life. On the other hand, I had to find a new member before the 'Smokers' would be so famous that people tried joining for the clout.

With the money gathered through the previous missions, I decided to select a driver for the group. Every day, I took taxis to travel from one side of the city to the other side and tried to choose the best one. Inside the taxi, I tried to look like a genius kid so that the drivers wouldn't feel as if they were talking with a child.

Nearly most of the taxi drivers talked about the 'Smokers,' and as usual, they tried to spread rumors and talk about things that were not true. Even if they did not speak, I brought up the topic. One of the drivers drew my attention. His name was Kevin, a 32-year-old man who looked very sociable.

"Some people accuse the 'Smokers' of firing at will. They are displeased that the 'Smokers' waywardly pursue to implement justice. They believe that it's the duty of the police to create peace and security for the city, but I really disagree with them," Kevin said enthusiastically. "When we talk about the 'Smokers,' I say there's no need to get a permit to do good works. I read in a newspaper that the man lying on the ground in front of the supermarket had confessed to the police that for the past three years, they had been making meth inside the supermarket." Kevin added, "If the police were efficient enough, they would have realized it during all this time. I would have surely helped the 'Smokers' that night if I was there. I don't know how, but I wouldn't let them work alone when they are doing their best to help the people of our city."

I finished our discussion in a simple way, and after getting to my destination, I got off the taxi, saying a simple thank you, and noted down his plate number. He said that he had told others about his ideas. That week, I assigned Mike to get in touch with him by any means and invite him to the group; as usual, I rolled a message to him and put it beside the notebook.

There was no need to convince him by using motivational quotations. The way he talked about 'Smokers' showed me that he could be trusted. Inside the fake cigarette, I wrote to Mike that for the next mission, he had to change Kevin's taxi plate number and the color of the taxi so that it wouldn't be tracked later. As Mike used to work in a car repair workshop, I assigned him to do it himself. After the mission, he also had to return the taxi to its previous state so that Kevin could carry on with his ordinary life.

Kevin's car was a Honda Integra. There were many of these cars in the city, so it was likely that he would not get caught. I didn't doubt for a second that everything would go right. I was just a little worried that because of their curiosity, the group members would get in touch with each other outside the group.

A week passed, and I saw the fifth fingerprint in the book. We had no problem for transportation anymore. Mike did his job like a piece of cake. Everything happened faster than I expected—life is like that. Sometimes, no matter how hard you try, you do not achieve. Now I could focus on Jacob. By the

way, I had to supply a few more masks and boots for the rest
of the members. I was certain that I wouldn't have to assign
David to take part in the operations of the group. He was the
big brain behind the operations.

I went to Walmart. They were out of the previous boots I got
before, so I had to get a few pairs of boots similar to them. I
even didn't know their shoe sizes, so I bought size 9.5 for all.
There were also no more masks of the previous model. Sam
oversaw the notebook and needed no mask.

I wrote for David to give up his mask because it was possible
that someone would find it in his room since his lifestyle was
messy. I also wrote to him to pass the mask to Kevin. Kevin,
in turn, had to pick his message from the pocket of the beggar,
go to the library, and get his mask. The one I bought from
Walmart, I kept with myself to give it to the new member.

On my way back home, I decided to go to the beggar and see if
everything went well. He had changed his shabby coat to a new
one. He had bought the new coat with the moneys that
members put in his pocket every time they went to him to pick
their messages.

I stood in front of him and wondered what to say. Money was
the language we shared! Like Al Capone, I whispered into his
ear that if he wanted to get more money, then he had to wear
that damned coat. He got a little shocked and turned around,
though he couldn't see.

He stretched out his hand to touch me. I kept clear from him
and said in an even harsher tone, "If you'd like to have a hand
to beg with, you better drop it and do what I tell you." He
seemed to be confused and made a little fuss. A few people
were getting close to us, and I had to do something so that
they wouldn't get suspicious. I took a 50 Dollar bill out of my
pocket and put it in his hand to make him quiet.

Those people were just a few steps away when the old beggar took my hand and began to make a fuss. I wondered if he was mute or if he had forgotten how to speak because he always seemed to be quiet. Things were not going well, so I pretended to hug him while talking loudly so people could hear: "Don't mention it! This is the least I can do for you. Take this money and buy something to eat."

The pedestrians curiously passed by. Once they moved away, I pushed him back while holding his collar in my hand and said, "Listen, you old man! I won't let you ruin what I've already made. You take this money and wear the damned old coat, or you'll regret it." I let him free. He seemed to have become a little afraid but gradually got quiet and started to touch the money I gave him.

Everything might happen, and he might tell others what he met. Anyway, I had other problems and didn't want to think about this one. I left and hoped he wouldn't forget what I advised him to do. It was as though unfinished things in my life had to do with the things outside the group, and the group itself was somehow protected from bad things! Maybe we were really blessed—who knows?! For the next few days, I totally forgot to go see the old beggar if he wore the old coat.

Almost every other day, I went to the place where Jacob was lost, hoping that I would find a clue. In the meantime, I went to the library to find out if any new suggestion was made or if anything happened in the group. In the suggestions' part of the notebook, David had reported tracking two guys who had planned to set two Baptist churches on fire two Sundays later. Later, I gathered that they intended to challenge 'Smokers' this way.

David had also noted that since Baptists believe in separation of church and state and also Baptists are severely opposed to alcohol and tobacco, they possibly accuse the 'Smokers' of being dependent on the Baptist church. I somehow could understand the reasons behind their beliefs. Our previous mission was an opposition to narcotics and the mission before that was based on setting fire to the coffee shop where they sold alcohol to kids. I had a feeling that they had been influenced by our group so they would turn their ideas into action like we used to do! For any hero there should be anti-hero!

I had to offer a reaction. It was possible that Sam would doubt me and wonder how I knew the answer beforehand. So, I left the library and returned a few hours later. In the suggestions part of the book, next to David's suggestion, I drew a burning cigarette, meaning that the tall man had a positive view on his suggestion.

I had no idea where to begin, but it seemed that David had planned everything in advance: the next week, the duties of every member were mentioned in the fake cigarettes, so Sam put them in the pocket of the old beggar. I opened and read them to see what was going on. The interesting thing was that all members were informed about Kevin, our new member. It seemed that they often checked to see the new fingerprints!

I wondered how informed David was about their operations, as he even knew which churches were to be attacked. Well those people who intended to do that were college students and it would be possible David heard about that in one of those college parties. Their plan, according to David, was to start the fire outside the tenth street Baptist church at eleven o'clock in the morning on Sunday, when people were attending the prayers. Following that, and before the people could show any reaction, they would set ablaze the First Baptist Church on N. Cedar Street.

But, the 'Smokers' operation was to defend the churches. Since it was possible that the two would be set on fire at the same time, Adam had to ambush the attackers at First Baptist Church, while Mike would wait for them at Tenth Street

Baptist Church. They had to stop the attackers with their baseball bats; then, they would spray our goal on the churches' walls.

It was mentioned on the fake cigarettes that Mike and Adam had to supply the baseball bats from two different places so no one would suspect them, and they apparently had prepared the bats out of their pockets and didn't expect the tall man to pay for them! Their mission said that they had to let the opposing group to do part of their job so that the people would find out about their ill intentions. After the opposing group poured gas on the churches' walls, Mike and Adam had to stop them before they set the gas on fire. Then, they both would go to the beginning of 10th street, and Kevin would first pick up Mike at 11:10 by his car, then he would pick up Adam.

I also wanted to be present at the scene. I decided to wait around First Baptist Church so that if anyone happened to see me, I would say I was going back from school because Rolla high school was exactly one street yonder. I think we were all excited because we had to do the operations in daylight and before the people.

It was Sunday, and I had been watching the church since 10 o'clock in the morning. At 10:30, a guy in black and the same mask and boots that I had already prepared got off a car. It was Kevin's taxi that had been repainted with the help of Mike last night. That's why I couldn't recognize it at first glance. The car moved away quickly after Adam got out and waited to ambush in a corner.

I deeply prayed to God that Adam wouldn't see me around the place. After a few minutes, another man wearing a white mask got out of another car. His mask was like the masks of the bank thieves. Anyway, it was the beginning of an adventure. He gently went to an outside corner of the church and picked up a jerry can. I realized that he had put it there before and seemed to be ready for an operation. Adam saw him, but he took no action.

The man poured some gas around the church and went on to write something on the wall. Adam acted wisely and started to spray on the other side of the church wall to save time. They both were busy spraying on the walls. The man finished his job quickly and took the lighter to set the church on fire while Adam was still spraying. I couldn't see my people in the church burn to death. I had to do something. Adam did not notice that.

I found a piece of stone from the street and threw it firmly toward the man to stop him. I made it. Right at that moment, Adam, who had finished spraying, put the spray bottle in his pocket and went toward the man. The man in the white mask tended to finish his job as quickly as he could. He lit the lighter. Adam ran toward him with a baseball bat in his hand. The white-masked man put the lighter down and took out his knife. Adam attacked him with the bat, but the man dodged him and stabbed Adam.

Adam screamed so loud that he drew attention of the people inside the church. Almost ten minutes had passed since the beginning of the operation. Adam was trying to pull the knife out, but the white-masked man didn't let him and stabbed more. A few people opened the door of the church. The man had to run away, so he released the knife handle; at the same time, he lit the lighter and threw it toward the church. As soon as he turned to flee, Kevin hit him with his car.

He quickly opened the car's front door and cried out loud, "Adam! Come before the street is filled with people." Adam, who was bleeding, moved heavily toward the car and got in. The three men immediately moved away. Adam forgot to take the baseball bat with him.

Flames were moving toward the church. All members of the 'Smokers' had left the place, so I didn't fear being recognized

168

by them. I went toward the church and tried to put out the fire, pounding my shirt that I had taken off on it in order to choke it.

Women and small children were running out of the church, and I, together with some other men, were trying to extinguish the fire. In a moment, when all people were busy fighting with the fire, I threw the baseball bat aside to hide it from them. A few minutes later, when the fire was almost put out, the police arrived. To my surprise, I saw the very person I didn't like much. Yeah! Sheriff John Barr!

This time, his eyes popped out of his sockets, but didn't say anything and just helped to return things to normal. Then, he arrested the white-masked man and placed him in the back of the police car. He, after taking care of everything, looked bitterly at me and said, "I thought you are not a Christian. What are you doing here?"

I answered like a polite and shy kid: "They are my people! In fact, I had to be at school to study together with my friends. On my way to school, I noticed the fire in the church and quickly came here."

John Barr stared at me for a few seconds and said, "Did you recognize those who were here but ran away?"

"No. When I got here, this man was lying on the ground, and the church was burning," I quickly answered.

He sighed deeply and said, "I wonder, kid, why you are present every time something bad happens in the city."

I replied with a smile, "Surely, I'm sinister and should lock myself at home!"

His tone changed, and he said with smile, "Take care!"

I asked him if he was informed about Jacob, and he said that he was still following the case and that the police had disseminated announcements, so that if anyone happened to see him, let them know. Then he got in the car and left there. I picked the baseball bat, hid it inside my shirt and immediately returned home. This time, I was sure John Barr would watch me more carefully.

I couldn't go to visit Jacob's family, though. I didn't have the time. I returned home. The next morning, I took 20,000 Dollars to the library for the members to get their share. Adam rested at home due to his injuries for four days. During the time, his father replaced him in the coffee shop. After he returned to work, he still seemed unable to walk normally.

I wondered whether his family had gotten to know about the incident and if anyone took care of him at home. Unfortunately, I couldn't get too close to him. Anyway, I had enough time to look for Jacob again.

AN UNINVITED MEMBER

All over the city, people were talking about 'Smokers.' This time, the group had saved people's lives in public. There was almost a state of insanity throughout the city. Everyone had formed a 'Smokers' group and tried to administer justice. The word 'Smokers' could be seen on the walls of nearly every alley in the city.

The children imitated the 'Smokers' and used to wear the masks similar to that Adam, Mike, and Kevin wore on the day of the church operation. I read in a local newspaper that seventeen people arrested by the police had confessed to be members of the 'Smokers' while I knew we just had five members in the group! Even some people ended in quarrel with each other, claiming that they were the real 'Smokers' and that the others were the fake ones!

The good thing about it was that we were less in danger of being recognized, and if anyone happened to see us in operations, they would think that we were possibly imitating the 'Smokers!'

For our next mission, we needed an armed person. I didn't want to play with the lives of my members. The next mission

171

could be more dangerous.

A few days later, I went to the library and saw Mike's message where he had suggested his cousin as a new member for the group. He had written about his competence and skills and about how he was trustworthy and could be a help to the group. He had also mentioned that his cousin was in need of money, and if he was accepted to take part in the missions, he might benefit from the money shared.

I didn't like his idea. They were relatives and could get in touch with each other. Even they could refuse an indisputable obedience of the group. Maybe, they had coveted to gain more money through the 'Smokers' and make a living for their families. I was aware that the farther the members were, the more impossible it would be to find out about the truth behind the 'Smokers.' Two days later, I went back to the library and drew the sign of 'smoking is forbidden' beside his message, meaning that I was opposed to his suggestion!

Occasionally, I went to the dirt road in Martin Spring to find a trace of Jacob.

However, one day when I went to the library, I found a rolled cigarette paper beside the notebook. I opened the notebook, and in the suggestions part of it, I saw a message from Kevin, where he insisted to introduce a guy who had previously been serving in the army.

Both sides of the paper were filled with some handwriting of a guy named Matt. He had introduced himself as a former member of the army and had mentioned that in part of his career, he was hospitalized after a car accident. Afterwards, he had gradually lost the physical power to run and was later disqualified to be a gun man or be in the army.

He was very disappointed and had lost his whole dream in defending the people as a gun man. Therefore, he was unwilling to attend the army again and was living a boring life until he happened to know the 'Smokers' and regained his enthusiasm to start an adventurous life again. He hoped to be accepted by the 'Smokers' so that he might have the chance to take part in operations with gun and defending the people.

I finished reading one side of the letter and thought that it might be a trap, but I changed my mind when I read the other side where Kevin explained how he had received the letter. It happened one day that Matt got into Kevin's taxi as a passenger and found the rolled cigarette paper on the back seat. Kevin had forgotten to burn my message was delivered to him by Mike after reading it and had missed it in the car. So, Matt had realized that Kevin was a member of the group. When he got out of the taxi, he took the paper with him and did not say anything to Kevin. Later, he began talking to Kevin about the information in the rolled paper and said to him, "Do you smoke cigarette or read it?"

Matt suggested to Kevin, not in a threatening tone, that if he wished the secret to be left unsaid, he had to try his best to pave the way for him to be a member of the group, too! I wondered if the whole thing was a plan by Kevin to introduce one of his friends Matt by using a different story than Mike, whom I had already rejected his request to add his cousin in the group. Maybe Kevin was pretending that Matt was a stranger.

On the other hand, we were really in need of an armed man who knew how to shoot a gun, for the safety of our members during operations. I didn't know Matt, so I informed David about his life story and assigned him to investigate about Matt and let me know. David didn't have to take part in operations and was in charge of decoding and doing research jobs and investigations. A short while later, he reported the result of his investigation on Matt, on the rolled cigarette paper, and not in the book and that was positive.

I returned to the library and drew beside Kevin's message of request, a cigarette fuming at one end. I also put a message next to the book, in which I had explained procedures for Matt's membership. Sam, as usual, had to put the message inside the beggar's pocket for Kevin to pick it up, and pass it to Matt the next time he met him. Three days later I found the sixth bloody fingerprint in the related part of the book. It means he read the book and new the rules and of course familiar with "tall man" Now, at least, I had a peace of mind that for our next missions, we would have a better safety for our members.

It was interesting to me that during the whole time, Once again Sam used to see me, but he didn't chase me so that he could reach to the tall man. I call it a belief. I did something that even the police wouldn't do it for him. Now, he was in a better financial situation, he had a job, and Mr. Smith didn't bother him any longer.

Matt wrote something in suggestion part as soon as he joined and explained that since a long time ago, he had noticed that a group was involved with the thefts in Rolla, but as he was ousted from the army, he had no motivation to try finding it out. He also mentioned that the 'Smokers' had instilled a new motivation in him. In fact, Rolla was a city with a high record of thefts, but since a specific thing was not being stolen, no one would think that the thefts were something organized.

Like the previous mission, I had no idea how Matt got a clue about the latter news. But it was important that the members obeyed their boss without meeting him; I, in turn, believed them with my eyes closed. The main reason behind it was that all members of the group trusted each other.

Matt had put a pile of documents beside the notebook in the library. I browsed them but could understand nothing. I passed them to David to have a look. Surely he could find their hideout location somewhere in Rolla. He also found out from the documents that a group of villains used to steal valuables of the people, store them in their hideout, and later dispatch them to be sold in other cities. Sometimes, they dismantled the stolen things and sold the parts separately.

It seemed to be a cheap job, but it was so flourishing that they could set up a team. I gradually understood that Rolla was not as calm and quiet as it seemed to be. I just had to look at it with more open eyes.

I asked David to study the case and report it to me, but he had misunderstood my message and thought I had ordered for the mission to be executed. The next week, he had made the rolled cigarette papers ready, indicating the duties of the members and put them beside the notebook. He turned to machine and was just ready to set up mission I admired his passion without laziness and delay. I was the first to read them before Sam would place them inside the beggar's pocket.

The location of the mission was somewhere in the city suburbs. The route to the place was a dirt road, and the wheel print of the car would remain on it. So, we decided not to go there directly and chose a longer road at the back of the location instead so that they wouldn't recognize the uninvited guests. The place of the operations included a big house with an adjacent warehouse among the trees. According to the operation's plan, we first had to pour some gas around the eastern side of the building, then one of the members would set a tree on fire to distract the people inside the house. We would then make our way among the trees to the north side of the building that had one window and was not so visible from outside. After the people inside the house would go out to put out the fire, we could figure out their total number, and right at that moment, Mike would go inside the building.

According to the plan made by David, all the members had to carry weapons with them. Matt had to supply the weapons. David had asked me which means "tall man" to leave enough

money for the weapons beside the notebook in the library so
Matt could get the weapons and train Mike and Adam two days
before the mission. I even did not bother stressing about them
training together and talking because I saw their faith on group
already how they were loyal to group and its rules. It seemed a
reasonable request. I put a few thousand bucks in an envelope
and left it beside the notebook.

Anyway, after Mike entered the building, he had to go upstairs
with a jerry can full of gas and set the whole floor on fire in a
way he would be surrounded in the flames and stop others
from going upstairs. In case of any danger, he could use his
weapon. Mike had 5 minutes for his part. In the meantime,
Adam would crawl to the ground between the house and the
people outside and had to place some traps so people's feet
would be caught in them.

The grass on the ground was high enough for Adam not to be
seen. Matt, too, who couldn't walk normally, would hide
between the trees and protect Adam and Mike with an air rifle.
None of us could use firearms to defend ourselves. Then, it
was Adam's turn to go quickly inside the house and scatter
some road spikes that are used to puncture car wheels on the
roads to confine the people to the ground.

Our estimated time for the operation was about 20 minutes.
Sam would call Phelps county police from a public call box at
12:20 p.m. to report them the address and run away from call
box. Kevin, at the same time, would blow the car horn to
signal other members of the group, and Adam would begin
writing our motto "Smokers protect people's properties!" on
the walls. Mike, who would be surrounded by the flames of
fire, would tie one end of the rope he already took with himself
to a spot in the room and would cling on to it to get out of the
only window to the north and reach to the ground. In the end,
all the members would go to the car and leave the place.

None of the members could use any telephones because of the

possibly being tracked. The means of communication were the rolled cigarette papers on people's lips. On the day of the mission, I didn't go to school; I went to the location of the mission instead.

I was there at 10 a.m. I took a sandwich from home for my lunch. I know it sounds foolish, but I needed energy. I heard Kevin's car and saw them arrive. The house looked very quiet. A short time later I saw the flames of the fire, the signal for the start of the operation sounded. I made myself ready. After a few minutes, I heard noises from inside the house. A few guys with buckets of water in their hands were running toward the flaming tree.

I saw Mike, with a rope wrapped around his body and a jerry can in his hand, enter the home very quietly. Adam placed the traps in the path between the house and the people. Everything was going well, but I was attracted by a clash on the second floor. For a moment, the gang turned their faces and saw Adam a few yards away. They stared at him in astonishment, but Adam didn't hesitate to run toward the building. The sound of something breaking was heard from the second floor. I hoped that Mike was safe.

The plan was somewhat disturbed. The group of gang members was going back sooner than we expected, and Mike had not yet set the floor on fire. I was just watching.

There were five people all together. Matt shot two of the gangsters with his air rifle. The third one's foot was stuck in the trap, and the other two were lucky to get themselves to the building. As soon as one of them opened the door, he stepped on a road spike. He shouted in pain, making the last one realize the trap and jump in the window.

I saw Matt walking toward the house, though it was not part of the plan. There were only the sounds of clashing. The second floor was ablaze at last. I saw the rope hanging out from the

177

window. A few minutes later, the whole first floor was filled with smoke. After shooting a few bullets, Matt got out of the house while carrying Adam on his shoulders. It seemed that Adam had got injured again. Damn it!

Mike, clinging to the rope, came down to the ground from the second floor and ran toward Matt and Adam. He took the other arm of Adam. At the same moment, one of the gangsters with a gun in his hand came out of the house and aimed at them. I didn't hesitate to immediately run toward him, jump on him, and make him fall flat on the ground. Then, I blew his face till he passed out.

The 'Smokers' didn't notice me or the gunman because the sound of fire and the people wailing inside the house. The mission was finished before Kevin could blow the car horn of the car as a sign of the end of the operations. The timing of our plan was disturbed. It was possible that the police and firefighters would arrive late, and a few persons inside the house would burn to death. They disappeared into the woods.

I couldn't get myself to the second floor through the stairs. So, I entered from a part of the house not covered filled with tear gas. Then, I dragged one of the mattresses in a bedroom to the outside of the house. I climbed the wall using the rope that was hanging from second floor, entered a room, and found one of the bad guys on the floor. I dragged him to the windowsill, wrapped the rope around his waist, and tied it firmly. I then pushed him out of the window and let him hang about one meter from the ground.

I saw Mike's spray bottle on the second floor and took it. I also found a few bundles of 100 bucks inside a half-open safe and picked them up. Then, I jumped down from the window on the mattress and began running away. While running, I noticed that the 'Smokers' had forgotten to write their motto with spray paint. I wrote the 'Smokers' sign on the wall of the warehouse that and quickly left the place.

I directly went to my workplace when nobody else was around. My school was finished, and I tried to behave normally.

UNDERGROUND

The next day, I saw the frenzied people who had realized from the newspapers and the police that their stolen things were found in a warehouse outside the city. The 'Smokers' turned into idols. I was sure that my group members, by seeing the motto sprayed on the wall, found that they were not alone and that a supporting force was present in the operations.

Next morning, I went to the library and left 18,000 bucks to be shared among the six members involved in the operations. I also put 3,000 bucks inside an envelope and skidded it under the metal front door of Mike's shop. I added a message for Mike to pass the money to his cousin who needed it. This way, maybe, I could pacify him because I already had rejected his request of membership, but I had given a positive answer to Kevin's demand.

The whole city looked at the 'Smokers' as heroes. I decided to temporarily stop the group's missions to focus my attention on Jacob. Again, I went to the same place where I had found signs of him. One of those days, I accidentally found something that made a sound different from the usual sound of walking. While I was walking around that area, stopped at once and stomped on it. It was as though I was kicking something made of wood!

I bent down and pushed some of the grass and mud aside and realized I was standing on a wooden door! It couldn't be: An underground way in the midst of the trees and far from residential areas! I even didn't ask myself what it was. I just opened it. It was very dark there. I went down a metal ladder while closing the door over my head. I couldn't see anything in the darkness. I put my hand in my pocket and touched Jacob's key ring.

I was lucky the key ring had a small flashlight on it to light up the space before me. I moved a little forward and lit my surroundings to see where I was. There was a table in a corner and a filled board on the wall. The place looked more like a hideout. It was not very large, and one could walk a few steps to reach the other end. A distance away, there was a desk with a computer screen on it and a few bundles of folders beside it.

I walked toward the wooden board and was busy watching the papers on it when a light from the ceiling was thrown onto the floor. I turned quickly and saw the door opening.

My heart stopped for a moment! I was surrounded and had no way to escape. The palms of my hands were soaked in sweat. The person who opened the door put his first foot on the ladder. The light from outside helped me get a better view of the place. There was no way to escape, and the best place to hide was under the computer desk in the corner. The desk was large enough for me to hide my whole body.

I abruptly went under the table and tried to breathe slowly. My heartbeat was so fast I feared the man would find me there. He closed the door, and the room became dark again. I could hear his footsteps. A few seconds later, the whole room lit up. Next to the ladder on the wall, there was the light switch that I didn't notice at first. I was very fearful of the evil he might inflict on me. I could see his legs from under the desk.

He went toward the board, and I could understand from the sound of the papers rustling. I was feeling better until he turned to me. I thought that he had seen me. I closed my eyes and heard a few sounds of click above my head; he had turned on the computer! I was lucky he didn't sit in the chair, as his legs would have hit me if he did.

He started to type something while he stood there. A short while later, the door on the ceiling opened again, and someone said, "Come on! Move it!"

The man inside the room said, "OK. I'm coming."

His damned voice seemed very familiar to me. I carefully looked at his shoes. They were brown dress shoes but not at all familiar. A few seconds later, he turned to the door and walked toward the ladder, but he didn't shut down the computer. He turned off the light and went up the ladder. The room became dark after he closed the door, but the light from the computer lit up the room a little. I waited for a few moments. After I heard a car starting up, I understood they had left the place.

I came out from under the desk and looked at the computer. The background picture on the desktop was the same circle with the 'X' inside it. I got it! The shape engraved on the trunk of the tree was not accidental. It was a sign to find this place! I had no idea what group or organization it belonged to. I turned on the light and went to the board. It was the map of Phelps county. On part of the map, I could see weird writings that I didn't recognize.

I wanted to take those papers with me, but I didn't risk the danger. There were other maps on the board, relating to different parts of Missouri. I took out my notepad from my pocket as always I had with myself and started to write those odd symbols. I quickly turned off the light, climbed the ladder, and opened the door above my head. When I was sure there was no one around, I ran toward my bike between the trees and rode home. I hoped they did not see my bike between the trees.

I put the papers under my bed beside the moneys. The next morning, I went to the library without saying anything to Sarah or even Sam to find the map of Rolla and Phelps county. I borrowed the maps, took them home, and tried to discover the mystery behind them. I knew I couldn't ask anyone about it, because Sam would question if the sign I used to prove my words earlier, had something to do with us. If he ever happened to read the book and realize the mission to disclose the same sign, he would understand that I lied to him that night.

The bad thing about lying is this: We usually begin with a small simple lie but later have to say much bigger lies to hide the first one! I worked on the map for a few days, but my attention was drawn by something unusual. The lines on the map I saw at the hideout were not exactly roads or rivers. Some of the lines were drawn by them to make special shapes.

The stranger thing was that the shapes in which the weird writings were written, looked familiar to me! I thought so much until I remembered that I had already seen those shapes in my geography classes. Yeah! Those were almost like the maps of countries. What countries, though? Wait a minute! The date written on one of the shapes was exactly the date of Jacob getting lost! No! It couldn't be true!

As I said before, Jacob was an African American. He was born in Ghana. I prayed that what I was thinking didn't come true. I looked at the desk globe my family had bought for my birthday. The shape formed by linking the lines was the same as Ghana's map! Jacob's getting lost was planned. The shape could be seen at the bottom right corner of Rolla.

Right at the top of Rolla's map, a date and location were written that tickled my fancy. It was about three months ago when Thomas got lost. The shape inside which that date was written resembled Chile! I heard that Thomas was Latino and from Chile. There was no room for doubt. A little to the left, at the top left of Rolla, I saw another shape inside. I realized who the fourth victim was going to be. I had to guess the country!

I got goosebumps once I saw the shape. I didn't need to compare it with the globe anymore. I knew that country very well! It was my own country that I was born in it. It was 80 percent like my homeland, and my homeland is not the same as any other country in the world! I was astounded my blood was frozen! I was their next target. I got an awful feeling. I sat on the floor and held my head in my hands.

I was thinking about telling the police, but I gave it up. The 'Smokers' were much more successful than the police, and I didn't want to endanger Jacob's life. Right there, I promised to save Jacob's life and surrender myself to the police and submit all the documents and inform about their hideout.

I couldn't mention the entire truth in the book, because if it happened, Sam would read it and notice the sign. I already had pretended, in a way, that the circle was a sign of our group. If he would realize that we were looking for a clue to find them, he would surely doubt everything, and considering that he was still young and unexperienced, I couldn't predict his reaction, especially when one of his friends' life was in danger.

I began to read the notes I had already taken and found out they were something like a tracking code.

I assigned David to continue examining the case, as I was unable to find out more. It was so complicated that even Sam would struggle to understand it.

The days slipped by, and I got closer to the time of me being kidnapped from unknown organization! A few days later, David came to me with a note saying that a consignment was to be delivered by Frisco railways in Rolla. He had decoded the date of the train departure and wrote it beside his note. I didn't hesitate to assign the group to a mission to rescue a boy named Jacob from the train. It was a sensitive but necessary mission.

Five days later, David made an exquisite plan, determining the duties of the group members. Because I was going to surrender to police after the operations, and wouldn't have access to the library, I managed to leave the money shares before the operations so the members would get their rewards in case of my absence. It was the reason why the 'Smokers' was formed from the beginning!

The whole group seemed to be ready because only after two days, there were no stickers on the back of the beggar's coat! It meant that all the members had already received their fake cigarettes.

It was late June, and a few months had passed since the first mission that we started together. I had enough time to concentrate on the most sensitive and vital mission. One day on my home from work, I was busy thinking about the aftermath of the upcoming mission. Suddenly, I came to myself and realized I had taken the wrong way home.

We had become so big and famous that our news was spreading throughout Missouri. People of most cities in the state had formed 'Smokers' groups and spontaneously defied corruption in their cities.

I really had no idea what would happen in the future. Frankly, the situation was not as ideal as I expected it to be. The discipline and order in the city were disturbed. Nearly everybody acted deliberately to gain his civil rights, and fewer people than before made their complaints to the police. Rolla was almost out of control, and there was chaos everywhere.

It's true that no one dared to commit wrong, but many people allowed themselves to reach fame under the name of 'Smokers' and embark on queer things. For example, they had set a supermarket on fire and sprayed the word 'Smokers' on the walls of the supermarket! The bad part was that because they thought they were doing those things to establish justice, they were not afraid of being arrested and tried. I even saw two groups of young kids quarreling with each other, and each group claimed they were the real 'Smokers!' Even if people were protesting about things in front of buildings or office, they were chanting, "Who cares? Smokers!"

SMOKERS

THE LAST CONFESSION

I saw this phrase also sprayed on walls in the streets. People really believed in us. I was engaged in thinking about these things, then someone caught my eye. The very tall man that gave me peace of mind was by me. The very man who somehow was the reason my group formed was in front of me. During the past few months, I didn't happen to see him at all, maybe because I was busy and distracted by other things. Anyway, I saw him and believed it could be a sign!

On one hand, I owed him all the good happenings in the past few months; on the other, I had intended to surrender myself to police after completing my last mission. In a moment, it jumped to my mind that he could be a proper substitute for the leader of the group. Why not? Throughout the story, I had introduced myself instead of him! 'The tall man'

I chased him to find his house. I made it. I then went back to the library and assigned Matt to meet and befriend with the tall man. Later, he had to arrange for a meeting between the tall man and I. I emphasized to him to set the date of the meeting

187

to be on the day of Jacob's rescue mission. Of course I did not mention he was the real tall man who inspired me and I just mentioned him as a future member.

A few days later, I saw the message from Matt in the 'Mission Description' chapter of the notebook: everything went as expected, and he could convince the tall man that he was a real member of the 'Smokers.' He also made him agree to hold a meeting with the leader of the group.

In addition, Matt had asked if there was a need for him to be a supporting force; in response, I rejected by drawing the sign of 'Smoking is Forbidden' beside his message.

Now all members of the group had the address of the tall man and could go to see the real man behind the adventures. It didn't matter to me, because I had already made up mind to surrender, and I was sure that this trick was now serious and would eventually disclose.

I offered to meet the tall man somewhere in the suburbs. I was thinking about the mission and the way I had to introduce myself to the tall man, then somebody knocked at the door. It was Jacob's family, who personally invited us to his gathering; yeah, I totally forgot about that.

The people were to gather in front of Jacob's house to light candles and sympathize with his family so they wouldn't feel alone. The date of the gathering was the same day of the mission. Jacob's parents face made me so upset. I couldn't see their disappointed face.

It was going to be a very busy day for me. First, I had to attend the gathering. Then, I had to take part in Jacob's rescue mission. Finally, I had a meeting with the tall man. The next day, too, I would surrender to the police if I didn't get kidnapped! I didn't have enough time to fear being kidnapped!

I was deep in my thoughts the day of the mission arrived. My family and I went to Jacob's house with lit candles in our hands. Nearly all the people of the city were gathering there. Sheriff Barr was attending, too! Two more hours were left until the beginning of the operations. Jacob's family talked to the audience about the hard times they had those days, then sheriff Barr started his speech. Sam had no role in the operations that night, so he could stay at the gathering.

Cody, Henry, and I were standing next to each other and looked disappointedly at each other. When sheriff finished his speech, he talked with some police officers and later came to us. I tried to behave normal. He told us how the city was dangerous and in chaos and advised us to be more careful. He even offered to show us a psychologist clinic if we didn't feel mentally well. Henry asked him for the address, but the sheriff had apparently left the visit card of the clinic at home. He said that he had the address in mind and asked for a piece of paper to write it on. Henry said, "Please wait. I will take a piece of paper from my mother standing over there."

I forestalled unintentionally and said, "I always have a piece of paper with me." I reached into my pocket and took out the notepad, but to my bad luck, Jacob's keyring came out with it and fell on the ground. At once, it went silent for a few seconds, and everyone stared at the keyring in astonishment. I couldn't swallow my saliva!

"This is Jacob's keyring. What's it doing with you?" Cody asked abruptly.

I was frozen. I started stammering and said, "Jacob gave it to me as a souvenir."

"When did he give it to you?" Henry asked.

"A few days before he got lost."

"But you told me before that you were not in talking terms with each other and that you hadn't seen him for a while,"

Sheriff said.

I had no reply. I just looked briefly at him and kept silent. The people around were looking angrily at me. I didn't know what to say. Right at that moment, one of the colleagues of sheriff came to him and whispered something in his ear. Sheriff glanced horridly at me and said, "Amir! I think we have to talk a little!"

His colleague said in an anxious voice again, "Sheriff! Please hurry. It's vital, and we have no time."

The sheriff, who seemed hesitated, said, "OK. I'm coming," He pointed at me and left us without a word.

They were giving me an evil eye and were suspicious of me. My face was as white as a ghost, and I didn't know what to say. As we were exchanging looks, the voice of someone talking drew my attention. Oh, wait! It was familiar to me. I had heard it before. Yeah! It was the hoarse voice of the man in the underground room. He was one of the school janitors. He passed us by and glanced mysteriously at me and at Jacob's keyring in my hand. I looked down at his shoes. They were the same brown shoes I was looking at the other day from under the desk in the underground room.

I turned and started to go away slowly. Henry called me, but I did not respond. The school janitor was getting closer to me with every step. It was a terrible situation. I was getting further away from the gathering. I had a feeling that he intended to kidnap me right there. It didn't seem to be a wrong thought. As he got closer to me, I became more anxious.

From among the mob, I started to run toward the alleys. I looked back and didn't find him there. Then, I looked around and saw a man on my left who was getting close to me from the next alley. As I turned back, I also saw my school janitor again. I didn't remember his name. I started to run away as quickly as I could. I didn't look back, either. I was just running.

I could hear their footsteps getting closer. I tried to go from one alley to another one so they would get confused and miss me. As I was wandering in the alleys, I became stunned. Oh my God! It was the same mute boy with his dog who used to appear before me in the worst situations! He was standing next to a garage door and was looking at me. Dimmit! I wondered how in the world he always tracked me and appeared before me. I was short of breath. I feared they would find me if the dog barked. I didn't know what to do. To my astonishment, the boy pointed with his finger to the door of the garage. I didn't have enough time to think whether to trust him or not. In fact, I had no other choice, because the alleys were so quiet that sound of my footsteps would draw them toward me. I went to the quite dark garage, and he closed the door behind me.

I was gasping for breath when I suddenly heard their voices from inside the lane. "Ask this young fellow. He might have seen him," one of them said to the other.

The school janitor said, "Hey kid! Did you see anyone passing by?"

I understood from the vague sound of the boy that he was trying to communicate with them.

One of the men said to the other, "Oh, this poor kid is dumb. If he happened to pass by around here, the dog would have barked for sure. You go that way, and I will go the other way." The sound of their footsteps faded, and I knew they left the lane. The boy opened the garage door a few seconds later. I wondered what to say to him. He was the one whom I hated the most, but now he had saved my life. I tried to thank him in his own language.

I had no more time and had to reach to the location of the

mission. I didn't have a mask, so I entered a shop that was closing, entreating the shop owner to close the shop a few minutes late. I bought a wolf head mask and went toward the railroad where the intended train was about to pass. I hid behind the trees. I could hear the approaching locomotive. Other members of the group were hiding around the place. I was informed about details of the mission and duties of each member in the notebook.

David, who already had decoded those mystifying writings, had informed me that Jacob was being kept inside the only blue wagon and was supposed to get to the destination by tomorrow. So, my men had to wait for the train to pass and jump into it once they saw it. Luckily, the speed of the train was not high when it passed Rolla. After rescuing Jacob, the members of the group had to jump off the train.

Adam, because of his recent injuries, was not capable of jumping into the train, so he would stay inside the car with Kevin to pick up the other men of the group for back up. David, who was an expert in computers, had manipulated the timing of the cross-section lights for Kevin so he would reach the place of the mission in due time. David was crazier than I knew. He was capable of way bigger missions by his talent, but sadly it may was my last mission working with them.

Mike and Matt were waiting near the railroad so they could hold onto a wagon door handle in the best time and get in the train. Mike had brought a metal stick with him from his workplace to open the wagon door lock. Matt was armed with a gun to defend against any uninvited guests!

The blue wagon was there, and they jumped into it. I, too, entered a few wagons back. The train was moving at a constant speed, and I was trying to keep my balance while holding onto a door handle.

The only way for me to move forward was to walk over the

roof of the train! My blood adrenaline was so high. I began crawling forward on the wagon roofs. The speed of the train was increasing. I could see my men. Mike struck fiercely at the lock of the blue wagon with the stick in his hand to break open the door. As soon as the door opened, someone kicked him out of the train! We just lost Mike, and I couldn't see where he landed since train was moving fast.

Matt, who was not wearing his mask until that moment, wore it and waited for the man who kicked Mike out to stick his head out of the window. Then he blew the man's head with the stock of his weapon, grasped his hair tightly in his hand, and threw him out of the train. As Matt was looking at the man rolling in the dust and stones, another person appeared in front of him, aiming his gun toward him.

There was so much noise that no one would hear me even if I shouted. By that time I was a wagon away from them and had no weapon to save Matt's life. It was a terrible moment. I just had to see Matt being shot with the gun but wait! I could do something!

Jacob's keyring was still in my pocket. I swiftly took it out and threw its light directly on the man's face, blocking him from seeing. He lost his concentration. At that moment, Matt came and noticed the light on the man's face. Then, he quickly shot him, throwing him out of the train. Matt turned his face toward me so he could see the one who had saved his life, but he could only see my wolf mask. He stared at me for a few seconds but surely couldn't recognize me. The rest of my body was not in his field of visibility, and so he couldn't tell if I was a teenager or an adult.

He went inside the wagon. I was waiting for him to see if the rescued person was Jacob. It was Jacob, but he seemed so weak and thin that it was almost difficult to recognize him, and his muscular body had considerably drained. Anyway, once I saw Jacob and Matt in good condition, I jumped out of the train.

My face and hands got injured a little, and I sprained my right leg. I hoped that Jacob and Matt would reach Kevin's car without any problem. The two men thrown out of the train couldn't be a threat to Mike. Mike had only suffered a kick from the man and was not even injured, so he could find his way to the city and I would not need to worry about him.

I had lost my way back home, but after following the rail tracks, I could find my way to the city. I was exhausted and didn't have enough energy to go to the place of appointment on foot. Finally, after a long run, I got to our ally where our house was located. I cautiously went toward the home but didn't go inside. I just took my bike which was parked in front of the garage door.

I didn't have a good feeling and felt like I was being chased by someone. My parents were certainly worried about me, because I had disappeared all at once and had not returned home. I didn't see anyone around, but somehow felt their presence.

With injured hands, I was hurriedly riding my bike to go to the suburbs. The place of appointment with the tall man was on the other side of the city.

It was very quiet everywhere. It was strange for a riot-torn city like Rolla to be so quiet. I got to the place of appointment. Feeling very thirsty and going dizzy, I waited for almost half an hour. He showed at last. He was driving a truck, and after getting off the car, he started looking around.

I went to him and said hello. The tall man took an astonishing look at my bloody appearance and seemed not to remember me at all. A vague silence prevailed for almost thirty seconds. I broke the silence at last and said, "I know it! You didn't expect at all to see a teenage boy here in front of you. Believe it or not, it's the truth! Before we get to start a Q & A game, let me tell all about my story from the beginning." Then I began to introduce myself and told about how I got to know him and the whole story.

The whole time, he was just listening to me with his eyes popped out of his sockets. After I explained two of our missions, he seemed to be convinced that I was not lying.

After explaining everything to him for about ten minutes, I added, "I've found a very wicked and dangerous group in the city I can't stand against them alone. The lives of many of my age-mates are in danger. I will surrender myself to the police tomorrow morning, but as you were the main cause of all those happenings, I sincerely ask you to accept leadership of my group. I know I made a chaotic situation in the city, but the important thing is that people have regained their belief in justice and good deeds. I'm sure that Rolla, a religious city, will continue supporting the group in establishing justice. In the beginning, I had the impression that nothing would happen in Rolla but later realized that this city is the center of all developments that are hidden in the darkness! You are the one who can return hope and brightness to this city and its people. You better know that the fame of the city has spread everywhere in Missouri now."

"The word 'Smokers' has seven letters, and we are six members. You can be at the head of the group as the seventh member! If you are displeased being the last letter, don't worry: in our mother language, the words are read from the right!" I smiled.

He was looking at me in a cold and senseless manner. I understood it was not the appropriate time for humor or, so I changed the issue by saying, "Anyway, tomorrow morning, I'll go to the police station with all the documents I have. It all depends on the 'Smokers.' Frankly, I never thought I would choose a person as my predecessor. It's a strange world. If I had not met you that day, I would have never reached here."

We stared at each other for a few seconds. He started to talk: "I still wonder if the things you kid said were merely a fabricated, but the day when you helped arrest the thieves, I became glad. You know, it was in one of these thefts that killed my unborn child. They took her necklace, and after police found the storage unit, I found the necklace there. The police and detectives could never track the thieves. Nothing in the world could make me glad except catching those villains. When the army man asked me for a meeting with the 'Smokers' boss, I was anxious to know who I had to thank. I never thought that a teenage boy was behind all those happenings."

I was happy to hear that. I never asked for his name, and Matt never mentioned it in the notebook. For me, he was always the 'tall man.' I was really feeling that some other people were present. I knew I was not alone. I could hear their footsteps. It was the sheriff who showed off at last and shouted, "freeze or I'll shoot!" I was sure he had chased me from the moment I got home so I would let him reach the man behind this story. I think he was right because he had caught me in the worst situations, and it seemed natural that he would question me after all those happenings; however, he didn't know that I was the founder of the 'Smokers!' He aimed his rifle toward the tall man because he had known him as the cause of all evils! And I had Jacob's keyring.

The backup police forces came out from the shadows of the trees. I was at the end of the rope, and nothing made a difference to me. I would have faced that scene eventually, but I still felt like there were people around us other than the police. Maybe, the school janitor who saw Jacob's keyring in my hand the other night had understood that I was aware of them, and since I ran away from him and his colleague, I could be a potential danger.

As the sheriff was getting closer to us, his tone turned graver. Suddenly, the tall man seemed to have seen something behind me and shouted, "Lie on the ground!" Then, he swiftly jumped

196

toward me and held me tightly in his arms. The sound of a bullet was heard, and I felt my body get hot. The tall man, whose name I even didn't know until now, turned his back to protect me from being shot and took the bullet. Still, one of the bullets hit my right leg. A few moments later, my whole body started to feel cold. Both of us were lying on the ground, and I was looking at the sky. It was dawn. It made me speak strange sentences:

"It's dawn. It's a damned dawn. The same dawn I always wished to see one day! I thought I'd begin a nice day by seeing the dawn, but this time, having seen the dawn, I finished my night all over filled with nightmare. In fact, not only my night, but my whole life! I've no idea how I got to this point, but I know I hate dawn. I hate this damned dawn till my last breath!

In the interrogation room ...

Amirhossein took a brief look at Jill and said, "Now do you understand what I meant by those words before I was arrested? That's the reason I hate dawn. The tall man lost his life to save mine. I was sentenced to jail for causing riots, disturbing the discipline of the city, and keeping illegal moneys. The police could not find any trace of the gang involved in human trafficking and was incapable of arresting the men shooting at us. The school janitor was declared innocent because of lack of evidence even though Thomas was never found; his case is still open. No trace was found of the underground room, and everything returned to normal after Jacob was found. Even Jacob did not remember anything when he was kidnapped. The members of the group were released after a while. To be clear, as you already know, Mike and Adam left the town. Sam is now a lawyer concerned with justice. Kevin continued his former job. David dropped out of school and is likely drunk in one of the bars. Matt opened a gun store. I'm here serving my sentence."

Jill, who was bewildered, said, "What a dramatic story! Though I've so far read your account several times, it's difficult for me to believe it. Everything in this story seems to be imaginary. Aren't you missing your family and your people?"

Amir smiled bitterly, bowed his head, and said, "As I explained throughout my story, I mostly used to watch the operations and only took a direct part when I found something imperfect. I'm not the right person to be asked about the imaginary or real nature of the missions. You must ask this question from the members themselves who were practically involved in all the tasks. To answer your question that if I miss anyone here, I have to say that occasionally, the people I know visit me. In the early days, when the 'Smokers' were at the top of the news, however, many people used to visit me often. Hmm! It's as though it's a museum here! My father comes and pay me a visit every week. I think he likes me more now than before. Anyway, more than anything, I miss my deceased mother"

At this moment, Amir became emotional, covered his face with his hands, began weeping, and asked Jill to stop recording his voice. Jill complied with his request to show her respect for him. At once, Amir stopped weeping and signaled with his head to the prison staff members in the room while staring at Jill through his fingers. One of the guard men immediately picked up Jill's recorder and cellphone off the table.

Jill became afraid and said, "What're you doing? Return my items!"

Amir took his hands off his face and said, "No worries! I must be sure that no one will hear what I say from now on. It should be a secret between us." Jill stood up, getting ready to leave, when Amir said, "Don't be afraid! I won't bother you. It was a long time since I began waiting for this moment. I can't leave here, but you can. So, I need your help!"

Jill said, "With what?"

Amir said, "Please sit down. I speak my words, and if you don't agree, we'll return your things." Jill looked at Amir and the prison staff members for a few seconds and sat on her chair. Amir continued, "I'm safer here. It's like my home. The 'Smokers' still live in the prison. I've lit a candle of hope and excitement in the heart of the people that they won't let diminish. When the 'Smokers' moved throughout the State, many people could obtain their rights. Here, the prisoners and staff members pay respect to me. However, if I ever had a way out of here, I wouldn't be able to accomplish my goal."

"What are you talking about?" Jill said.

"Whatever you recorded was the truth. I said the same things elsewhere, but I didn't say everything. The day I went in the underground room, I found a folder and took it with me. I've hidden it somewhere. It's not hidden at the library or under my bed or anywhere that anyone could find it. It's been a long time since I have known you, and I'm sure you're in a position to help me. Believe it or not, this interview had already been arranged by me! I ordered my men outside here to talk to your magazine's manager and arrange for an interview. I've to tell you that the group whose sign is a circle with a letter 'X' inside it is a highly clandestine organization who kidnaps humans from every race to perform horrible experiments on them for their secret projects."

"What projects?" Jill said.

"I wish I knew. The only thing I know about them is that they're located in a forbidden area—an area that everyone has heard about but not seen!" Amir said.

"Do you mean Bermuda triangle?" Jill asked in astonishment.

Amir smiled in a devilish manner and said, "Don't go too far! Much nearer than places like that! I'll let you know the place where I've hidden the folders. What I request you to do is decode them and try to find their goals. You've to know that people like Thomas, Jacob, and I are being kidnapped by them to become their lab rats, and no one is able to track them."

"Why didn't you inform the police?" Jill said.

"Throughout time, many kids have been kidnapped, and no clues were found. This is our only chance to accomplish the 'Smokers' mission. Here, I write the address. Don't forget: You don't have to trust anyone or talk to anybody," Amir emphasized.

Amir wrote the address on a piece of paper and gave it to her. After a pause, Jill took the paper and put it in her purse. Amir pointed to one of the men to return Jill's things. Jill, a little shocked, took a brief look around, hung her purse on her shoulder, and moved toward the exit door.

In the meantime, Amir shouted while laughing in a strange manner, "I hate dawn! I've always hated it, though I made it happen! Ha, ha! I love this damned dawn!"

Amir, while lighting a cigarette, looked at Jill. She was still frightened as she left the interrogation room, thinking of where the story may go next. She had not a clue but knew that it was certainly not over.

….. to be continued!

Made in the USA
Monee, IL
28 May 2022

97152834R00115